# THE FANTASTIC ORDER OF ODD TRAVELERS

SHERRY TORGENT

BLUE INK
PRESS

Copyright © 2022 by Sherry Torgent

Published in the United States by Blue Ink Press, LLC

ISBN-13: 978-1-948449-12-0

Library of Congress Control Number: 2021950280

www.sherrytorgent.com

*Cover Illustrations by Gavin Churchill*

*Coloring by Laura Hollingsworth*

*Cover Design by Cassie Torgent*

...SECURE COMM TRANSMISSION TO TRAVELER #2520 FROM THE FANTASTIC ORDER OF ODD TRAVELERS

...URGENT

...PORTAL DETECTION: NORTH CAROLINA MUSEUM OF ART

...DEPLOY IMMEDIATELY...PROCEED WITH CAUTION...ROGUE PIGGYBACK RIDER DETECTED...

...MISSION: SECURE TARGETS

...13:15:03 INTERSTELLAR TIME

# PART ONE

## ABIGAIL

T
oday was Abigail Hawk's birthday—lucky number thirteen. She now had the privilege of calling herself a teenager.

Big whoop.

She didn't see *any* benefit to the label. Pimples, popularity, body image angst, more homework. None of that sounded very appealing. But this was the age where she should be breaking through the paper tape of the finish line of adolescence. She had survived childhood! She was moving on to phase two. But instead of relief, there was a lingering knot of worry sitting and festering in her stomach like a bad burrito. She needed a plan to get through all the ages that ended with "teen" without a blip on the woe-is-me radar.

It was true that some of her past plans to improve her life hadn't fared so well.

Learning to be a hairstylist by practicing on her Barbie's hair.

Fail.

Building a cabin in the backyard so she could have some privacy.

Fail.

Starting a blog about building a cabin in the backyard.

Double fail.

But *this* new plan was going to work. It was going to be her greatest feat, her coup d'état (a fancy French word for over-throwing the government, which sounded a lot like what she was getting ready to do with her teen years). The plan was solid. She hoped. Because by far, her greatest fear was that she'd end up being one of those teenage girls who cried into her pillow at night because she had no friends.

Because currently she didn't.

Have any.

Friends.

"Abigail! Let's go!" her mother yelled up the stairs.

She quickly stuffed her cross-body bag with all the essentials—journal/sketchpad, water bottle, and phone. She wrapped a blue checkered scarf around her neck, even though it was September, because it made her feel more European.

She tied back her frizzy blonde hair and sighed. Today was the day she would begin her plan to become an artist—one where she'd travel the world with her own exhibit and laugh at the jokes of millionaires clamoring to buy her art while she sipped expensive mineral water collected from an ancient spring.

She closed her eyes and smiled, savoring the thought.

"Abigail! I have a manicure appointment! If you want me to drop you off, we have to leave now!"

Abigail stomped down the stairs hoping her mother would hear the anger in her steps. She didn't exactly blame her mother for the divorce, but her mother's decision to pack up the SUV and move her and her two older sisters across the country to Raleigh, North Carolina was the reason Abigail had to concoct a stupid plan to begin with. How else was she to cope with having no friends on her thirteenth birthday?

Well, she shouldn't say she had *no* friends. Technically, she had one. But she wasn't sure he counted. His name was Daniel. She'd met him at the North Carolina Museum of Art last weekend when she was mapping out her I'm-turning-thirteen-seven-year-plan-to-avoid-adolescence-and-become-a-famous-artist plan.

Daniel was thirteen. Maybe. She wasn't sure, and for some reason it hadn't come up. Their first meeting had been...strange.

She'd been standing in front of a contemporary painting when a boy approached and stood beside her. She'd only taken notice of him because he had been wearing a baggy jacket over a black vest and collarless white shirt that was loosely tucked into his tan pants. It looked like he'd pulled out clothes from a dusty trunk he'd found in his grandparent's attic in an old farmhouse in New Hampshire.

The meeting had gone something like this:

*"This one's not worth a fart in a whirlwind," Daniel said with a snicker.*

*Abigail looked over at him like he was a dead rat the family cat had left at the door.*

*"Oh, excuse me," he said upon seeing her expression. He stood a little taller, pushed his shaggy brown hair out of his eyes, and cleared this throat. "This picture has existential value, don't you think?" He rubbed his dimpled chin in contemplation while holding a small red book over his heart.*

*The book may have been his most secret thoughts, or just as*

5

*likely,* something he carried to complete his attempt to impress *people.*

"Do you even know what that word means?" she asked. Because she didn't know what it meant, and she wanted to be impressed with his knowledge of such a big word, but at the same time, she was thinking he was 100% crazy and was just making up nonsensical garbage.

He looked over at her with his steely blue eyes and lifted his chin ever so slightly.

"Existential. E-x-i-s-t-e-n-t-i-a-l. Existential is a philosophical way of thinking. It sees humans with will and consciousness as being in a world of objects which do not have those qualities."

First, she did a quick translation in her head of what she thought the word really meant. Humans possess something the world around them does not.

Second, she scanned the room to make sure she hadn't inadvertently walked into a spelling bee. There was no one else around except for a security guard dressed in the museum's uniform—royal blue polo shirt and black pants. He seemed to take account of them with unbiased professionalism.

Abigail considered walking away, but since this boy had just given her a new word she hadn't known (and yes, she had a thing for words), she pursed her lips and countered with the intention of being disagreeable instead.

"No. I don't think it does. Have existential value." She let the word roll off her tongue as though she had used it hundreds of times.

He raised an eyebrow. "No?"

Abigail folded her arms, tucking the museum brochure she'd been carrying around under one arm. The arm folding was her defense mechanism whenever she felt uncomfortable.

There was a brief awkward silence, and then he laughed. And not just a chuckle. He slapped a knee with his hand and howled. For

6

*some reason, this angered her. She glanced over at the guard. He was picking at something in his teeth with his tongue.*

*"What's so funny?" she snapped.*

*He wiped one of his eyes with the back of his hand then grinned at her.*

*"I'm Daniel," he said, extending his hand.*

*Her only thought at that moment was*—no, you're weird.

*She shook his hand like it was a bit of toilet paper she'd just pulled off the bottom of her shoe. "Abigail," she said warily.*

*Her lack of enthusiasm didn't seem to affect his good humor.*

*"It is a pleasure to meet you. Have I seen you here before? You look familiar."*

*"No," she said flatly, though she'd been to the museum last week with her mother, and it was likely that he* had *seen her. She couldn't help but feel like she had just been the brunt of a joke, and she wasn't quite ready to be best buds.*

*He opened his jacket so she could get a full view of his vest. "You probably don't remember seeing me because I'm often in disguise."*

*She debated at this point whether she should just walk away. Honestly, isn't that what most people would do? But the situation was akin to standing at the edge of a pool of freezing water. She didn't really want to jump in, but a part of her wanted to show how tough she was. No wimping out.*

*Abigail sighed, though she masked it by releasing it slowly through her nose. "And why do you disguise yourself?" she asked, bracing herself for a long explanation which she'd already decided was going to be ridiculous.*

*"My mom works here," he said. "And frankly, I get tired of being recognized by her cohorts."*

*She stored the word cohort in her mind vault, deducing that it meant coworker.*

*"Oh Daniel, how you've grown," he said in a high-pitched voice.*

*"How handsome you are young Daniel." He fluttered his eyelashes. "Don't you have a girlfriend yet?"*

*He rolled his eyes.*

*Abigail smiled and unfolded her arms. Now this was something she could relate to. Her mother's long string of friends were equally annoying. Normally, they gushed over her frizzy blonde hair, and told her how lucky she was to have hair with so much potential. Inside she'd be cringing because she hated her hair. It was so thick and unruly it could have had its own zip code.*

Anyway, that's how Daniel and she had become sort of friends. She didn't even know what school he went to or what his last name was. That's why she wasn't completely sure he counted as a real friend, but he would have to do because she needed someone to spend her birthday with. Otherwise, she would have been stuck with her mother's idea of a celebration, which would no doubt amount to her mother inviting her new adult work friends and asking them to bring their kids to stand in as Abigail's friends.

*No, thank you.*

The only hiccup in her birthday plan was that she'd let it slip to Daniel that today was her birthday. The fact that she was choosing to spend it with him at the art museum wasn't exactly her proudest moment. But a girl had to make do with what she had. He'd said he was going to plan a big surprise for her at the museum. She had told him no gifts, and he'd assured her that what he had in mind was better than any gift. She hadn't asked him to explain.

That was a huge mistake.

# CHAPTER
# TWO

Abigail spotted Daniel pacing in front of the gleaming white West Building of the art museum. He was wearing the same old clothes he'd worn last weekend along with a flimsy cap like someone from a Dickens novel would wear. He was tipping his cap and saying good morning to everyone who passed him until he spotted her.

"Abigail, over here," he yelled, waving his arm in the air.

She scowled as she drew closer. "Really?" she asked, surprised to see him in the same ancient clothes.

"There's a reason, I promise," he said.

"You look like you just stepped out of a Dickens novel."

"Who is Dickens?"

"You know. *A Christmas Carol*?"

Daniel blinked a few times with wide-eyed curiosity.

"God bless us everyone?"

"Hmm," Daniel said, seeming completely clueless.

Strangers were casting sideways glances as they walked by Daniel. "People are staring," Abigail said.

"How do you know they're not staring at you?" he said with a wry grin.

She grabbed his arm and led him toward the large silver doors, anxious to hide him from curious eyes among the many galleries.

"Your shirt is quite the eye-catcher," he said as they entered the museum's white halls. "What do the initials stand for? M-E-H?"

She stopped. "You're kidding, right?"

He shrugged.

There was something different about Daniel that she couldn't put her finger on. His lack of knowledge of pop culture was worth raising an eyebrow over, not to mention his strange choice of clothes.

"Meh," she said, "means, I'm not impressed. Or, I don't care. Take your pick. It's indifference."

"Oh," he said, his voice deflating.

"What's wrong?" she asked, wondering if he had taken her words the wrong way.

He scratched his cheek. "Nothing."

"I'm just not excited about turning thirteen. My shirt has nothing to do with you, okay?"

"Very well. There's nothing to be done about it now." He strode off past the information desk.

She jogged to catch up. "So...what's the big surprise?" she asked cheerfully, trying to brighten the mood.

"You'll see."

She dug into her bag and pulled out her new leather art journal and a pencil. It had been the only birthday gift she'd asked for. A ship was etched on the front—perfect for chronicling her plan to sail through her teen years.

*Ooo, metaphor.* She gave herself a mental pat on the back.

*Day 1,* she scribbled at the top of the page while she walked.

"What do you think of Rodin?" Daniel asked.

She looked up. They were standing in the midst of Rodin's Court. Auguste Rodin to be exact—a French sculptor. The museum held one of the largest collections of his bronze statues in the world. The court was a sea of dark, twisted torsos, hands, and faces—a virtual graveyard of black-bronze monuments.

Daniel stepped up to a statue of a nude man and waited for Abigail to study it. The sculpted man's whole body was bent backward as if he had just been struck. One knee was down, embedded in what looked like a large stone. She read the placard.

*The Falling Man.*

She didn't know what Daniel was expecting her to say, so she remained silent.

"It's a version of the man clinging to the underside of the doorway of Rodin's sculpture *The Gates of Hell.* He's trying to escape the fire," he said.

She glanced over at him, wondering what this had to do with her birthday surprise. A black contorted figure in distress wasn't exactly what she'd had in mind. She was thinking more of the painting *The Garden Parasol*—a woman of leisure in the serene setting of a French countryside garden taking tea and reading poetry under a bright yellow parasol.

"Does this *freak* you out?" he asked.

He'd said the word freak like he'd never used it before and was trying it out.

"No. It's just a statue," she said, still thinking of how splendid it would be to sip tea in a French garden.

"Good," he said taking off.

She scrambled after him, shoving her journal into her pack.

"Where are we going? I want to actually learn something about art today."

"Oh, you will," he said.

He held open a door that led to an outdoor courtyard and bowed slightly, gesturing with a sweep of his hand for her to go first.

Abigail rolled her eyes at his attempt at chivalry. She stepped out onto the gray graveled courtyard known as Rodin's Garden. A handful of life-sized sculptures of men were positioned around a long, rectangular reflecting pool bordered with river rocks and filled with water lilies. The word that came to her mind was zen-like.

"Come on," Daniel said, hurrying toward the far end of the water feature.

She reluctantly followed. She'd rather be inside writing something brilliant about an art piece. She wasn't up for Daniel's game. If this *was* a game.

He stopped at a statue at the end of the garden. The sculpture was of three nude men, slightly hunched with their heads touching as if they were conjoined. Their left arms dangled in front of them; their right arms were held by their sides.

"Did you know that all three men are identical?" Daniel said. "They only look different because they're turned at different angles. It's the only sculpture ever done this way."

"Wow, you're right," she said, walking around the statue. The three men all had the same face, same muscular arms and legs—like bodybuilders. "Why are they looking down?"

"Rodin designed them to stand at the top of *The Gates of Hell.*"

She eyed the men's oversized feet. "So, they're supposed to be what? Guarding the...gate?"

Daniel laughed a little. "Not so much guarding it as warning those who are about to enter."

She studied their sad, dejected faces.

Daniel continued. "On the final piece, these men are at the top pointing down to the inscription above the doorway. *Abandon hope, all ye who enter here.*"

"That's kind of creepy."

"These men represent the dead."

"So, the sculpture inside that you showed me?"

"You'll find *The Falling Man* on the side of Rodin's *Gates*."

"Wow," Abigail said, lifting the flap of her bag. "You really know how to throw a birthday party." Finally, she had something interesting to write about in her art journal.

Daniel reached out and stopped her. "Not yet," he said.

Abigail sighed. "Daniel, I want to write this down."

He held up a hand. "Just...please wait."

"Fine," she said, closing the flap of her bag.

He took out the same red book he had been carrying last weekend and read something from it silently, then stuffed it back into his pocket. He then held out his hand to her, waiting for her to take it.

She scowled. "Daniel, I don't think we're that kind of friends."

He grinned as if she'd said something ridiculous. "Just for a second. Trust me, I'm not trying to win your affections or anything."

His response, though weirdly formal, was more insulting than trying to hold her hand. "Why aren't you trying to *win my affections*?" she asked, "What's wrong with me?"

"You're..." He seemed to be struggling to find words. "I'm too old for you."

"How old are you?" she asked.

"Thirteen?" he said with a grimace.

"We're literally the same age!"

"It's hard to explain. But you'll understand soon enough."
He stood there resolutely with his hand still extended.

She sighed and took his hand. He glanced over his shoulder, clearly making sure they were alone. She was ready to knock him in the head if he tried to kiss her. But he didn't. He squeezed her hand tightly and said in a voice that sounded like church bells announcing the midnight hour, "Through me is the way into the doleful city."

"Dan—" her words were cut off by a blinding light and a feeling of falling. Her stomach dropped like she was plummeting on a roller coaster.

*What is happening? Am I passing out?*

Her body plunged through darkness and light in a kind of nauseating, endless spiral. But just as quickly as the feeling of nausea had come, her senses began returning one by one.

Feet. On solid ground.

Daniel's warm hand. Still in hers.

A whiff of animal, straw, and salty sea air.

Face. Warmed by the familiar touch of the sun.

She blinked. Her vision slowly returned, expanding from a small pinprick into brilliant light. She was...

*Somewhere else?*

Daniel released her hand. They were standing on a dirt road lined with buildings that were made of plaster and wood and had thick, thatched roofs. It was like they had stepped back into medieval times. A weathered piece of wood, nailed to a post, indicated they were standing on *Shoe Lane*.

"Daniel," she said slowly.

"Surprise!" he said, with weary enthusiasm.

The heat of fear rose from her neck to her face. "Where...*are* we?"

Daniel removed his cap and scratched his head. "I'm not sure exactly. Not yet anyway."

She grabbed his arm and squeezed with all her might. "What do you mean you're not sure?"

"Ouch," he said, pulling away. "Calm down. I'll figure it out in a minute."

"Figure what out?" she exclaimed.

Daniel slowly turned in a circle and took in their surroundings. "If I were to guess, I'd say we landed somewhere in the 1300s."

Abigail swallowed and eyed the old-world style buildings and dirt streets. Multiple flags were flying atop the buildings that lined the street. The flags were a faded royal blue and were dotted with yellow markings that looked kind of like an iris flower—fleur-de-lis she believed the symbols were called. Seagulls called to each other in the distance.

"I'm dreaming," she said to herself. "This is one of those dreams inside a dream where you think you're dreaming and then you realize you're not, but you have, in fact, been dreaming the whole time—"

"Oh no," Daniel said, interrupting her.

"What?"

"I hope I'm wrong, but I think we might be in Calais. The flag has the colors of the French crown. And if I'm right, the sound of seagulls means we're on the coast."

"Where's Calais?"

"France."

*Calais, France*
*August 3, 1347*
*Jean de Fiennes – with Pierre & Jacques de Wissant*

J ean stood with the Wissant brothers in the town square with the rest of Calais, anxiously waiting the governor's arrival. The Wissant brothers, much older than Jean, had taken him under their wing after his father had died. He appreciated their kind gesture, but he was eighteen and perfectly capable of living on his own—not that what was going on in Calais could be called living. Their French town had been under siege by King Edward's English army for the past eleven months. The city's wells were drying up, and food was as scarce as the rain. Some nights, when things grew still, he could hear the distant laughter and music of the English army camped outside their city walls. Those were often the same nights when a light ocean breeze would carry a whiff of boiled potatoes or hot goose fat dripping into a fire. Those faint smells would wrack Jean with pains of hunger so severe he'd have to spend the rest of the night in his bed with his knees drawn to his chest.

"What word from the governor do you suppose?" Pierre Wissant asked, rubbing a hand through his short hair.

"I'd say he plans to surrender," his older brother Jacques said. "I don't see that we have a choice now that our French king has abandoned us. Almost a year we waited for the brute, while we've all wasted away to skin and bones. And what does he do? The great King Phillip leaves us to fend for ourselves."

Pierre nodded solemnly.

Jean kept silent. He had no fight left in him.

"Mark my words," Jacques continued. "If England takes Calais, the rest of France will fall, and all Frenchmen will be bowing to the whims of England."

Jean stared vacantly at his dirty bare feet. He'd forgotten to put on shoes.

Pierre, the brother who had taken on more of a fatherly role with him, clasped Jean on the shoulder. "Why don't you come by the house, after this. We don't have much, but Henrietta is still laying a few eggs, though I fear her days are numbered."

"You name your chickens?" Jean asked, finding this sentiment strange in the midst of a starving city. Everyone who raised and killed animals knew not to grow attached by naming them.

Jacques grinned and held up a finger. "Correction. He has one chicken."

Pierre ignored his brother. "She's alone now and naming her is the one bit I can do for her, scrawny thing that she is."

"Not that it will do *Henrietta* any good," Jacques said. "He'll have her on his table soon enough."

Pierre smiled and gave Jacques a friendly push.

Despite his inner emptiness, Jean smiled too. He didn't realize he was still capable of doing that. It warmed his heart to hear the Wissant brothers carrying on with each other in the midst of such a crisis. It showed their good natures, and it made Jean glad to be in their company.

Suddenly the crowd tensed, and murmurs spread. Jean and the brothers stood on their toes. The governor was taking the platform to speak. Now they would hear the fate of their beloved city of Calais—fight on and starve, or surrender their home to England's King Edward?

# CHAPTER
# FOUR

"FRANCE!" Abigail shouted, but then she immediately flew into denial. "Hah, hah. I hate this dream." She pinched herself over and over, but she couldn't wake herself up. She checked inside her bag. Everything she had packed that morning was safe and secure. It didn't look like she was dreaming.

Her breathing quickened.

Daniel took her gently by the arms. "You need to breathe."

She nodded and took a deep breath and blew it out slowly.

"We've traveled to the past. Rodin's sculpture, *The Three Shades*, is a gate—a portal to the past."

"Uh huh," she said, still unable to comprehend what was happening.

He released her and stepped back. "I wanted to surprise you for your birthday, though I had been hoping for another time period—clearly."

She took a tentative look around. There were shops with signs hanging above them, but every door was closed and the curtains drawn. No one was on the street. It was like one of those western movies where the cowboys ride into a town and tumbleweeds bounce down the abandoned dirt streets.

"This isn't possible," she said.

"I felt the same way the first time I time traveled," he said.

She widened her eyes. "You've done this before?"

"Once," he said, removing his hat.

"I want to go back," she said matter-of-factly.

He grimaced and scratched his head. "It's not that simple."

The blood drained from her face. She unwound the scarf from around her neck and balled it up in her hand.

"Don't worry, we'll get back," he said, pulling his red book from his back pocket. "We just have to find the return portal."

*Portal?* Abigail's breaths came shorter and faster.

"Ahh. Here it is," he said. "*Calais, France - watchtower. Should be easy enough to find.*" He crammed his book back into his pocket. "I mean, a tower is kind of hard to miss." He grinned at her sheepishly.

*His red book is for time travel?* She pressed her scarf to her mouth for fear she might scream.

Shouts rose in the distance.

He popped his cap back on, gently took her wrist, and led her toward the voices.

"Are you sure this isn't a dream?" she asked, alarmed.

"If this is France," Daniel said, ignoring her panic. "They'll be speaking French, but you'll hear it in English. It's some weird phenomenon of time travel I guess."

*Time travel?* There were those words again. This was definitely a dream.

*I'll eventually wake up. Won't I?*

Along the way, he insisted that she cover her "Meh" T-shirt, so he grabbed a discarded grain sack and ripped holes in it for her head and arms and helped her slip it over her head.

"Perfect," he said. "You'll blend right in."

Now she had bad hair and clothes.

*Yep, this is a dream all right. A nightmare.*

They rounded a corner and the town opened up into a large, cobblestoned city square. A mass of cheerless, haggard people—men, women, and children—were standing in front of a wooden platform that looked like it doubled as a venue for public hangings. The wooden beams, empty of ropes, stood as reminders of what was in store for would-be criminals. But what was happening now was clearly not a hanging. An older man with white hair and a long matching beard stood singularly above the crowd. He was wearing a black velvet cap and a long, tailored jacket that looked too big. His face was thin and gaunt. His eyes watery and troubled.

Daniel pointed at a tall tower across the square—their supposed way home.

"Fellow citizens!" The man called out in French, though she understood him just as Daniel said she would. "We are at a crossroads. Our wells are running dry and we have little food left. King Edward has blocked all attempts by our fellow countrymen to smuggle in provisions."

The man's voice carried with authority, and the people paid rapt attention.

"The English king has cutoff our supplies from the sea and land. Our French king, Phillipe, has been unsuccessful in freeing us."

"Uh-oh," Daniel said.

Murmurs traveled through the crowd, dying off as the man on the platform raised a wrinkled palm.

"What?" Abigail asked.

The man continued. "We should be proud Frenchmen, because our enemy has been unable to breech the walls of our fair city all these months. Our walls may be holding strong, but walls will not feed us. Walls will not fill our wells. Without the hope of rain or food, we will perish. We have no choice but to surrender to King Edward."

The crowd erupted.

"If we surrender, they will kill us!"

"Surely King Edward will show us mercy!"

"We'll die before we give our city to the English swine!"

"Listen to our governor!"

Men who disagreed with each other jostled and spat threats.

Daniel pulled Abigail closer to him in a brotherly, protective way.

"Daniel, what's going on?" she cried out.

The governor called out for order from the stage, but by now, multiple tussles had broken out.

"We are literally in the history of Rodin's sculptures at the museum," Daniel said. "What a floorer."

*A what?* Abigail's stomach twisted.

Men in triangular hats and tan knickers pushed through the crowd with swords dangling in scabbards at their hips and attempted to break up the skirmishes.

"What history?" Abigail shrieked above the crowd noise.

"The burghers of Calais!" Daniel said with a sense of awe.

"Burgers? Like hamburgers?"

Two men throwing punches fell at Abigail's feet. She gasped and clutched her scarf to her chin.

Daniel pulled her back while city soldiers appeared and pulled the fighting men up by their collars and drug them away. The shouts stopped one by one as the flames of anger were doused by the soldiers and order was returned to the gathering.

But calm almost always precedes a storm.

A strong hand landed on her shoulder, and another on

Daniel's. She and Daniel shared a look of puzzled shock, then turned and met the dark eyes of a woman with a jet-black ponytail. She was wearing a black belted jumpsuit and didn't look like she belonged in the war-torn town.

"You two, come with me," she said sternly.

The woman led them away from the crowds with a firm grasp on the back of their necks.

Daniel caught Abigail's eye and motioned subtly to the right with his head. "Time to wake snakes," he whispered. She had no idea what he meant, but she hoped this was his way of saying he wanted to make a break for it.

Her stomach twisted with fear. She nodded just enough for Daniel to know that she was in. The next thing she knew he was mouthing, "Wake."

Then he blurted out, "Snakes!"

They broke away from the woman and took off, away from the crowd and back into the narrow streets of Calais.

Abigail's scarf unfurled in her hand and trailed behind her like a banner. The woman was in hot pursuit, but Abigail and Daniel were kids; they could slip into places she couldn't.

"Come on," Daniel screamed as he pulled farther ahead of her.

Her bag was slowing her down, so she reluctantly tossed her bag and scarf and pushed harder.

*There's no place like home.*

The fabled words of Dorothy from *The Wizard of Oz* rang through her head. All she needed now to make her nightmare complete were winged monkeys flying overhead, chasing them.

They ran through hilly streets, crooked streets, and streets so narrow she wasn't sure they qualified as streets. They ran until they hit a brick wall—literally. Huge yellowish walls stretched their way around the city and were taller than the tallest of ladders. From what little medieval history she knew, in this type of walled city, there was no way out except through a city gate, which no doubt, in time of a war, would be locked up tight.

They were trapped inside Calais.

# FIVE

They stood panting, staring at each other. "Who was that woman?" Abigail asked breathlessly.

"I don't know, but in case you haven't noticed, there's a war going on between the French and the English," Daniel said, as if that explained everything.

"Oh, I noticed," she retorted. "But did we really have to come all the way to Calais to get a burger?"

Daniel frowned and shook his head.

"B-u-r-g-h-e-r-s. The burghers are men of prominence in the city. A large number of the sculptures in the Rodin collection at the museum are men from this city."

She put her hand on her hip and gave her ponytail a toss. "I knew that."

"Did you?" he said, looking skeptical.

"No," she said, deflating.

She really did have a lot to learn about art *and* history.

She filed away the word burgher and prominence in her word vault—though she couldn't imagine ever needing to use those words again.

Ever.

With the strange woman in black MIA, they calmly set out and navigated several narrow streets in hopes of working their way back around to the watchtower.

"Wake snakes?" Abigail asked, feeling naked without her bag and scarf.

"Yeah. What about it?" Daniel asked, peering around a corner before they ventured down another empty street.

"What exactly does it mean?"

"Oh. Um...you know, to get into mischief."

"A normal person usually just counts to three before doing something crazy."

He looked over at her and squinted. "Why would you count?" he asked, clearly missing the point.

"Never mind." She was too tired and cranky to explain.

Finally, after endless dead ends, they emerged on the other side of the town square very close to the large stone tower.

There was no sign of the woman in black, but the square was still full of people, so there was no way to know if she was lurking nearby, waiting. Daniel had said he didn't know who the woman was, but Abigail found it odd that he had dismissed her question about who the woman was so quickly. Didn't he want to know what the woman wanted and why she was dressed so strangely? Abigail pushed the thoughts away. She needed to focus on getting home.

"So, this tower is the way home?" Abigail asked, straining her neck to peer up at the tower. It had to be at least one hundred feet high.

"That's what the book says."

"You mean your *time travel* book?"

"Yes," he said impatiently.

Seagulls were perched silently at the top of the tower like curious spectators.

"Why this place?" she asked.

"The portal's location has to also exist in the current world," he said as he headed for the tower. "At least, that's my current theory."

"This watchtower still exists?" she asked, stunned that something hundreds of years old would still be standing.

Daniel removed his floppy cap and twisted it in his hands. "Well, a version of it still exists. Obviously not in this pristine state."

She sighed. *I'm in a country over six hundred years before I was born, caught in a war between people who are technically dead, and now I'm going to return home through a watchtower that at this moment exists in France.* The thought made her dizzy.

Daniel put a reassuring hand on her shoulder. "We'll be home in two shakes of a lamb's tail."

He grinned.

She stared at him in disbelief.

"What?" he asked.

"No one says that."

"It's an idiom. It doesn't mean to literally shake a lamb's tail. It just means we'll be out of here quick. Because you know...a lamb's tail shakes quick."

"I know what an idiom is, Daniel. I'm telling you that no one under the age of eighty says stuff like that anymore."

The enthusiasm faded from this face. "Oh."

"And what's a *floorer*?" she asked.

He gave her a blank stare.

"Back there, when you said we were in the history of Rodin's sculptures at the museum, you said, 'What a floorer'."

"You know...something shocking," he said, kicking at an invisible rock.

She crinkled her eyes. Daniel didn't act like someone who was thirteen. He dressed weird and used strange words. And now, with all this nonsense of time travel, she was really starting to wonder about who he really was.

"Daniel, is there something else you want to tell—"

"Oh no," he said, interrupting her. "Woman in black is back."

She followed his gaze. Sure enough, the mysterious woman had just shown up across the square, and she was glaring at them. They ran to the tower door. The door had a little window on it with bars and a large iron-ringed handle, the kind you'd imagine seeing in a medieval dungeon. Daniel dropped his cap and grabbed the handle. He tried pushing and when that didn't work, he tried pulling. Surprisingly, it squeaked open. The woman was running straight toward them.

Abigail shoved Daniel through the tower door. They pulled the door shut, enveloping them in cave-like darkness. There were no torches of fire attached to the walls like she'd imagined there'd be. As soon as their eyes adjusted to the darkness, they raced across the smooth stone floor to the flight of wooden steps.

"Are you sure this is the way home?" she asked uncertainly. Because if it wasn't, they would be trapped at the top of the tower with nowhere to go.

"Only one way to find out."

She grimaced. "Just go," she said, not wanting to be the first up the creepy stairwell. The creaking of the watchtower door echoed behind them. "Go!" she screamed. Suddenly she was wishing she'd agreed to her mother's birthday party. If she had, she'd be home right now, stuffing cake into her mouth and lamenting her lack of friends. Normal stuff. Thirteen-year-old stuff. Not this.

Daniel took two steps at a time, and she followed suit. They spiraled, making turn after turn until finally, a glimmer of light poured down from above. She could hear the seagulls perched at the top, calling out. A hint of fresh air cut through the damp smell of stone.

"Almost there," Daniel managed to say in a wheezy voice.

*I could be home eating pizza and crying into my cake.*

The simple pleasures of her tortured life flashed before her, fueling her to go on. Her legs burned with fatigue. The light above them grew brighter until finally they reached a door. Daniel shoved it open with a grunt and they stepped out onto the tower's balcony. A handful of gulls flew away as they stepped up to the railings. Outside the city walls of Calais, a large English encampment spanned all the way to the ocean where hundreds of boats anchored in the harbor. The English people moved about their makeshift city like ants in a very large colony.

"Oh my..." Abigail gasped.

The woman in black's boots echoed behind them, drawing closer and closer.

"What now?" she asked, refocusing.

"I say the same thing I said to get us here, and we'll be back at the museum."

"Well say it!" she screamed with one eye on the doorway.

Daniel took her hand and opened his mouth.

But before he could speak, two soldiers rounded the other side of the tower and surrounded them.

"Hurry, say it!" Abigail screamed.

"I can't, or they might come with us," he said softly.

Abigail's stomach dropped.

*I'm never going to see home again.*

# CHAPTER
# SIX

There had been no sign of the woman in black on the way back down the tower. The meeting at the square had finished, and the platform, where only moments ago the governor had spoken, was empty.

They were led through the streets by two soldiers, while the men, women, and children of Calais watched with shallow, worn faces from their doorways. They stared without feeling, their dusty clothes hanging from their bony shoulders.

*These people are starving,* Abigail realized. The governor had said in his speech that the English had cut off their food supplies, but she'd been so concerned about herself, she hadn't fully understood the predicament of Calais until now. She looked away, unable to meet their sorrowful eyes. What had become of them all those years ago? Daniel seemed to know something about this part of history, but they hadn't exactly had time for him to give her a history lesson. He'd been strangely quiet since their capture and walked stoically without looking at her. There would be no "waking snakes" this time.

Their journey through the streets ended at a small iron gate that led to a stone house with wide windows and a tiled roof. They walked through the courtyard which held the remnants of a past garden that now lay bare and weedy. One of the soldiers marched up to the front door and knocked. A woman in a soft, white cap and a long, brown dress opened the arched door and stepped back.

The soldiers prodded them forward, none too gently. They followed the woman to a room down the hall on the right. The woman scowled at them, motioned them inside, and retreated. The soldiers took their positions by the door.

The man with the white hair who had been speaking to the crowd just minutes ago sat behind a small wooden desk, lightly tapping a feather pen on a blank piece of paper. It took him a moment to realize someone had come into the room. He glanced up at them over his small spectacles, then removed them and stood, motioning them forward. Despite his haggard look, the governor towered over them.

Abigail's legs trembled.

The man narrowed his weary eyes and frowned. "I'm Jean de Vienne, the governor of Calais. But you knew that already, didn't you?"

Abigail glanced over at Daniel, waiting for him to say something, but he remained silent.

"I see," the governor said, sitting. He locked his bony fingers together and rested them on the desk. "What did King Edward hope to accomplish by sending in children to spy for him?"

Abigail's heart raced.

*He thinks we're spies!*

Daniel didn't flinch.

The man studied them. His gaze was not friendly. "Are you denying it?" Jean asked. "You were heard speaking English."

Abigail looked over at Daniel pleadingly. *Please say something.* But he remained silent.

"We're not spies," she blurted out.

Jean gave a thin smile.

Daniel sighed.

"Tell him!" she said to Daniel.

"Yes, young man," Jean said frostily, "tell me."

Daniel's face reddened.

*Why is Daniel mad?* Was she missing something?

Finally, Daniel spoke. "If I can have a minute with my friend, I'll tell you everything you want to know."

"If it's going to mean we can move your little charade along, then as you wish," he said dismissively.

Abigail followed Daniel out of earshot. "Do you have any idea what you've done?"

"We aren't spies!" she snapped. "We can't just stand there and let him accuse us."

He took a deep breath. "The first page of the red book says *beware of changing history.* We have to be very careful. The more we say and do, the greater the chances."

"So, we just sit back and let them hang us as spies?"

"They're not going to hang us."

"How do you know?"

"Because all of this has already happened. Don't you see?"

She didn't see.

Daniel rubbed his face in frustration. "Look. Think of it this way. A small pebble thrown in a pond can cause ripples that move across the whole pond. You just threw a pebble, and the pond is history. Change one thing here, change all of history."

That actually made sense to her, and her anger subsided. "I'm sorry. I wasn't thinking. Now what?"

"We do the best we can to make sure this all turns out like it's supposed to. Don't worry, I'll make up a thumper."

She had no idea what a thumper was, but now was not the time to ask. They returned to the governor.

"King Edward threatened the lives of our families if we didn't agree to spy," Daniel said.

*Ah. A thumper was a lie.* She fought the urge to store it in her word vault.

Jean nodded. "Well at least you're not denying you're spies," he said with a sigh. "I suppose we could spend time discussing how you got in and what your mission is, but all of that is pointless now. I'm sending a letter to King Edward to negotiate the surrender of Calais." He picked up his pen, dipped it in a small glass bottle of ink, and tapped it lightly on the rim.

Daniel glanced at Abigail and smiled. Relief washed over her. It was clear by Daniel's reaction that this was what was supposed to happen. They waited in silence as Jean finished the letter. He dipped his fingers into a small dish of sand, dusted it over the letter, and then lightly brushed it off. The letter was folded twice and sealed using wax from the single candle that burned on his desk.

Jean stood and handed the letter to Daniel. Daniel looked at it like the man was handing him a venomous snake.

"Take it," Jean said, giving it a small shake. "You and your friend are going to deliver our terms."

Daniel's face turned bright red, but he took the letter. Clearly, they weren't supposed to be the ones to deliver the letter, but what choice did they have? Ten more soldiers joined the ones who had escorted them to the governor's house, and she and Daniel were marched through the streets like common criminals.

Daniel held his chin high, but she wasn't feeling as confident. If they were sent outside the city gates, how would they get back to the watchtower so they could return home? Was it really wrong for her to think only of herself? Technically, everyone around her was already dead and gone. But even as she had the thought, a touch of guilt made her cheeks flush.

"Why does England want Calais?" she asked.

"Because King Edward has claimed the throne of France, and Calais is a perfect landing point for his troops. Once he takes Calais, he can replenish troops by sea and conquer the rest of France."

"Wow. I guess I should have paid more attention to history. This seems like...a big deal."

Daniel looked over at her. "A big deal?"

"Yeah. You know, a big deal—something really important."

*Doesn't know what a big deal means. Uses words like floorer and thumper.*

Daniel's hand tightened around the governor's letter. "Let me do all the talking."

"Right. No pebble throwing."

Despite her nervousness and her new curiosity about Daniel, she couldn't help but feel a certain fascination about being on the front lines of history.

*Thank you, Rodin. You're now my favorite sculptor.*

She tried to temper her excitement. They still had to get back home, and it wasn't always easy to be optimistic when you were thirteen.

They turned onto Tanner street and there it was: the city gate—a mammoth-sized door flanked by a castle-like tower structure. Abigail's stomach turned cartwheels. She had no idea what would happen to them once they were outside the city walls and in the hands of the English. Some of the soldiers ran ahead and lifted the heavy wooden braces that barred the large doors. Abigail and Daniel were getting ready to walk into the enemy's camp. Alone.

# CHAPTER
# SEVEN

T he lure of witnessing history firsthand evaporated as soon as the city gates began to open. Metal grinded against chain as the heavy iron gate behind the wooden doors slowly lifted and the drawbridge lowered over the moat.

A burst of sunlight poured into Calais. Abigail shielded her eyes with her arm.

Two French soldiers nudged Abigail and Daniel forward, across the bridge. Below their feet, underneath the bridge, was a deep chasm of water. Between the wide moat and the height of the city walls, no man, or army could have breached the fortifications of Calais.

On dry land, the English camp stretched as far as the eye could see. The camp was a mix of tents and wooden buildings. People milled about everywhere tending to the chores of daily life. The sounds of the makeshift city were lost to the beat of her heart pounding in her ears.

Three Englishmen on horses rode swiftly out of the camp toward them. The French soldiers shoved her and Daniel off the end of the bridge and then returned to their city fortress. The drawbridge creaked and groaned as it rose and disappeared back into safety. She fought the urge to cry as the chains tumbled, and the iron gate of Calais closed with a bang.

There was no going back.

She glanced over at Daniel. He stared straight ahead, but his hand had tightened around the governor's letter to King Edward.

Abigail studied the men riding toward them. Two of them were wearing mail armor over tunics and bowl-shaped helmets. One of these men carried a white flag with a red cross. She guessed that was the flag of England. The other carried a flag that had a checkerboard pattern of four squares on it. The red squares had gold lions on them, and the blue squares had white fleur-de-lis on them like the French flag.

"Why does one of the flags have the French symbol on it?" she asked.

"King Edward has claimed France," he explained. "The flag is a symbol of both of the kingdoms—Lion and Fleur-de-lis—Red and Blue—England and France."

Abigail swallowed. They had landed right in the middle of a war, and she had no idea what was supposed to happen next.

The small entourage of horsemen was stately and imposing. The man riding in the middle stood out as he wore no armor or helmet. He was strikingly blond, clean shaven, and tall by comparison to the men riding with him. The leather strap that crossed over his black tunic held a large sword that rested against his right hip. He rode with an air of confidence on a fine horse whose mane and tail glistened and moved like black silk.

"Who's that man in the middle?" Abigail asked.

"I'm guessing the king's son, Prince Edward. Later, history will remember him as Edward the Black."

She cowered slightly as the horses came to an abrupt stop in front of them. Edward was young and handsome. He couldn't have been but a few years older than herself. Heat rose to her cheeks.

The prince raised an eyebrow upon seeing the paltry party of two teens. Then he mumbled something to the soldier next to him and they shared a small laugh.

"I guess they were expecting someone else?" she said quietly to Daniel.

"Probably."

Prince Edward dismounted.

Daniel stepped forward and handed him the letter then spoke with a perfect British accent. "The governor of Calais wishes to discuss terms for surrender."

"You're English?" he asked in an amused tone. When Daniel didn't say anything, the prince's eyes, which were a piercing blue, flickered over to Abigail.

"Yes, we're English," she said in her normal 21st century voice.

Daniel shot her a look of displeasure.

She shrugged.

"I don't recognize your accent, my lady," the prince said with the slightest hint of a smile on his lips.

Daniel cleared his throat and continued with his British accent, "She's a cousin from a remote village."

Edward nodded and eyed Abigail's sackcloth shirt. She bit her lip and blushed.

"Very well, let's deliver your message to the king, though I doubt you'll find him willing to discuss *terms*." Edward chuckled and motioned to his soldiers, and they immediately circled behind her and Daniel. Prince Edward walked in front of them, leading them into the camp while holding the reins of his horse.

There were actual streets, though they were a mix of wooden planks and brick laid in sand. After passing by a long row of tents and prying eyes, they walked through a market in full swing. English vendors, trying to sell their wares, shouted to browsing soldiers. Smells of animal mixed with spices and the salty air reminded her of the petting zoo at the state fair.

A portly woman with a large mole next to her nose held up a live flapping chicken by its feet. "Fresh chickens!"

A man in a white shirt and black jacket stroked a piece of material folded over his arm. "Fine linen!"

"Fresh blades!" Another man shouted out as he sharpened a large silver knife across a stone.

It was as if the English had settled the French port like new colonists. It was impressive, but her admiration was quickly replaced with a deep sympathy for the people trapped inside Calais. Food was abundant on these streets, while the citizens of Calais starved.

Those who noticed the king's son passing through stopped and bowed reverently, giving little attention to Abigail and Daniel.

Abigail inched closer to Daniel. "Why do they call him Edward the Black?" she whispered.

"It's believed it's because he wears black armor in battle."

"Battle? But he's so...young."

"His father, King Edward III, took the throne when he was fourteen."

What would it be like to be a knight or a king while battling acne? Not that Prince Edward had acne. He was just about perfect as far as she could tell.

"It would be better if you didn't talk. *Cousin*."

Daniel's tone hit her wrong.

"Do I need to remind you that it was *you* who got us into this whole mess," she answered sharply.

Prince Edward glanced back with a curious eye. She wiped the frown from her face and smiled at him.

Daniel shook his head.

As they moved deeper within the camp, more wooden structures appeared. Even the people's clothing turned more colorful with tailored gowns and jackets. The common clothes of the merchants and soldiers had been left behind for the finery of a royal household.

Women and young children hurriedly carried baskets of bread and trays of food down the street. Men and boys groomed horses in a stable. Others were committed to the task of hanging laundry. One man standing by a row of caged birds fed a small fish to the falcon perched on his leather-covered arm. Abigail's mouth fell open in amazement.

Prince Edward stopped in front of what had to be the largest house in the camp. The house had a pitched roof, making it tower above the rest of the wooden buildings. It also had shuttered windows which could be opened to catch the ocean breeze.

*This must be where the king lives.*

Her mouth went dry. The guards at the door snapped to attention upon seeing Edward's approach.

The makeshift palace wasn't anything overly ornate, but its huge arched doors made from honey-colored wood revealed its occupants. Each door panel contained a carving of a lion raised up on two legs.

A young boy took the reins of Edward's horse and disappeared around the corner. The guards opened the palace doors to Edward, and she and Daniel followed obediently. Their footsteps fell softly upon a rich red rug, while candles burned above them in an iron chandelier.

A portly maid hurried forward and curtsied before Edward. He smiled and winked at her. She turned and led them down the hall. Daniel looked over at Abigail with a look of disgust as if he were making some point about the character of the Black Prince.

The maid announced Edward's presence inside a door to their right, and they were ushered into a room richly appointed with upholstered chairs, rugs, and a large wooden table covered with parchments and books. There was even a working fireplace, though winter had long passed, and the fireplace had been swept clean.

A bearded man rose from a chair by the fireplace and closed the book he'd been reading.

Abigail gasped.

*The English king!*

# EIGHT

King Edward's red hair poked out from underneath his jewel-encrusted gold crown. His black velvet tunic was embroidered with the silhouette of a gold lion. Multiple gold rings adorned his fingers, and velvet slipper-like shoes embroidered with a gold crest graced his feet. The king filled the room with his majestic appearance.

"Father," Prince Edward said. "Calais has sent a contingent of two children."

"Teenagers, actually," Abigail said, unable to resist the urge to correct the prince.

The king frowned as Prince Edward chuckled.

She blushed and added, "Your Majesty." She attempted a curtsey which she was sure looked as awkward as it felt.

Daniel shot daggers at her with his eyes. He bowed to the king but said nothing.

Prince Edward passed his father the letter from Governor Jean de Vienne.

King Edward swiped a sharp letter opener off the nearby table and sliced beneath the wax seal. He was quiet as he read the letter. His face visibly colored, making his red hair and beard more pronounced. He tossed the letter on the table and glared at her and Daniel. "So, they want me to spare their lives?"

He laughed, and Prince Edward followed suit like they were sharing some inside joke.

"They lost that privilege when they refused to surrender months ago," the king added. "I shall do with them what I wish." He paused as if considering the options. "Death comes to mind."

Abigail glanced over at Daniel. She had no idea what was supposed to happen next. Did the king end up massacring the people of Calais? Her hands trembled.

Quite abruptly, a woman entered the room. A tall, beautiful woman with a white headdress and brown braids curled into loops by her ears. Her long, white gown glimmered and flowed about her feet as she crossed the floor to the king. She had a pronounced baby bump.

"My darling, Philippa!" he said with open arms. "The governor of Calais has sent his messengers. We are about to conquer Calais at last. I promise to make their deaths quick and painless."

The queen didn't look quite as enthusiastic as the king. She turned and gaped at Abigail and Daniel. "They're children!" she said.

Suddenly, feeling self-conscious about her frizzy hair and grain sack shirt, Abigail lowered her eyes.

"You," the queen said after a moment of contemplation. "Come with me." The queen skirted by her as if she expected her to follow.

Abigail exchanged confused looks with Daniel.

The queen turned at the door. "It's not a request."

Abigail took a tentative step toward her. The king sighed,

and Prince Edward grinned as if he'd found the whole scene between his parents amusing. Before Abigail knew what was happening, she was whisked off to Queen Philippa's quarters in the back of the palace. The queen waved off her maids and guards and closed the door to her room behind them.

Abigail took in the queen's chamber with a reverent awe. The vaulted ceiling made the room feel much larger than it actually was. Though it was on the small side, the room was ornately decorated with rich materials and fine furniture. The bed itself looked like a throne with its golden coverlet and blue and gold satin canopy.

Beside the bed sat a basin of water and a linen towel. There was also a separate sitting area by a fireplace that included a wooden cradle for a baby and a small table that held a gold pitcher and a tempting assortment of dried fruits and nuts. Two large leather chests sat in a corner with a stack of books on top of them.

"Don't dally, come in," Queen Philippa said.

Abigail stepped onto a rich blue rug, worrying that her shoes were too dirty to be doing so.

The queen poured something into a gold goblet and handed it to Abigail.

She *was* thirsty. A small sip wouldn't hurt. She accepted the cup and chugged it. It tasted like bitter grapes. She stifled a burp and handed the cup back to the queen.

"More?" the queen asked.

Abigail shook her head. Her stomach rumbled, but the queen had moved on to pacing. Abigail would have eaten shoe leather if it had been offered to her. She hadn't eaten since breakfast. Dried fruit and nuts never looked more appealing.

"We have a dilemma," the queen said.

*Dilemma.* Abigail knew this one. *A difficult or perplexing situation.*

43

"King Edward has lost a great deal because your governor has refused to surrender for these many months."

Abigail held up a finger. "He's actually not my governor."

The queen spun to face her. "You're English?" she asked.

Abigail remembered what Daniel had said and tried to stick with the story. She couldn't fake a British accent. "Remote village."

"How have you come to be in Calais?"

Abigail froze. *Don't throw a pebble into history.* Daniel's words echoed.

"Orphaned and sent into service for a distant relative, Your Majesty." *Wasn't that in some Dickens novel?*

"I see," she said, not altogether looking convinced. She rung her hands. "Tell me the conditions in Calais."

"They're starving, and their wells are running dry."

The queen scowled and rubbed her round stomach. "We must play this right or the whole city will be slaughtered."

"Couldn't you just talk to the king?" Abigail suggested.

The queen looked at her like she was a naïve child. "He has every right to put the citizens to death. They broke the rules of a siege."

"There are rules?" *This is one strange world.*

"I will suggest a compromise. It's the only hope they have."

There was genuine concern in the queen's eyes. Despite the fact the English were unwanted invaders, Abigail liked the queen.

Queen Philippa nibbled on a fig. Her brow furrowed. After several awkward minutes of deep thinking, she summoned her maid. A girl of similar age to Abigail entered and curtsied.

"Where are Isabella and Joan?" Queen Philippa asked.

"Outside at the horse stable visiting the new colt."

"Fetch me one of Joan's dresses for Abigail. Something simple."

The maid bowed out of the door.

"Before we go back to the king, I'd like to make you more presentable."

Abigail's face flushed. "Philli—" She stopped herself. "Your Majesty. I'm fine. Really."

"You're wearing a grain sack. And your hair—"

"Is awful, I know."

The queen smiled. "Dear, I was going to say it was splendid."

"But it's frizzy." Was she really discussing her hair with the Queen of England? This was the best dream. EVER.

"It's unruly to be sure, but curly hair is a good fortune to the woman who possesses it."

Abigail's throat tightened, and a wave of emotion took over. She rushed forward and wrapped her arms around the queen's bulging waist. It was probably completely inappropriate, but no one had ever made her feel as good about her hair as the queen had.

"There, there," the queen said, patting her back lightly. "All will be well, you'll see."

Suddenly realizing that embracing the queen felt wrong, Abigail backed away, aghast. "I'm so sorry. I don't know what came over me. I read somewhere you're not supposed to touch a king or a queen."

"Nothing to be sorry for. I have nine children. I'm quite used to it."

Abigail gulped. *Nine children and one on the way?* Oh yes, times had changed.

The maid entered with a cream-colored dress and a corset. It wasn't anything fancy, but it was far nicer than her current sack.

"Sponge her down, dress her, and braid her hair," the

queen said to the maid. "Meet us in the king's lounge when you're done."

"Yes, Your Majesty," the maid said with a quick curtsy.

Abigail was going to court.

Well, sort of.

# CHAPTER
# NINE

Being treated like a princess on her birthday was beyond Abigail's wildest dreams. That is, once she'd gotten through the awkward scrub down by a maid who wasn't much older than herself. She hadn't had a sponge bath since she was a baby, but somehow it made the whole process feel...royal.

The maid combed out Abigail's thick hair and braided it in some elaborate design that Abigail would never be able to duplicate. Not that she had a mirror to see it, but she could touch it, and the weave was unlike anything she'd ever tried.

The dress fit her, thankfully, though the maid tightened the laces of the underlying corset with the strength of a man twice her size. Abigail's outfit was completed with a pair of soft shoes that reminded her of ballet shoes.

Daniel was going to freak when he saw her. Her little meeting with the queen could be a *huge* ripple in the lake of history. But there was nothing to be done about it.

She did feel a little guilty about enjoying her time with the English queen while Governor Jean de Vienne was back in

Calais nibbling off his yellowed fingernails. He was waiting for her and Daniel's return with the hope of King Edward's consent to spare the town's citizens. But she had no idea whether that was going to happen.

The maid, having completed her work, handed Abigail off to a guard outside the queen's room, and Abigail was ushered back down the hall to the king's lounge.

The queen was seated in a cushioned chair by the fireplace and stood immediately upon hearing the door open. Daniel was sitting on a stool by the tall, narrow table. He nearly toppled over when Abigail entered the room, but Prince Edward righted him with a hand.

"There now, isn't that better," the queen said, floating over to Abigail.

Daniel gaped at Abigail's attire. She couldn't tell if his red face was from too much sun or if he was boiling with anger.

She avoided his gaze and smiled at the queen.

"Thank you, Your Majesty. It's—" She tried to think of a formal sounding word. "Lovely."

Queen Philippa turned Abigail toward the king as if presenting her. Perhaps this was part of the queen's plan—to remind the king that Calais wasn't just men and women, that there were children there too.

"I'm guessing there's a point to this display," the king said, then yawned.

"Yes," the queen said. "A child shouldn't be wearing a grain sack. It's...immoral."

"Calais will be destroyed, regardless," King Edward retorted.

"Unless..." she said.

"Unless, what?"

"You were to show mercy."

The queen rested her hands on Abigail's shoulders.

Abigail glanced at Prince Edward. He smiled and winked at her.

Suddenly, the door flew open, and two teenaged girls with long, fair hair came barging into the room in their fancy dresses and shoes.

"Father, the new colt—" They both spoke at the same time then giggled.

The taller of the two girls spoke first. "She's beautiful, Father."

"She has a bit of white on her nose," the other daughter said.

"Can we have her, Father?"

All of the king's defenses dropped, and he wrapped one arm around each daughter. "If my Isabella and Joan want the new colt, then they shall have it."

The girls, who looked to be a bit older than Abigail, put their hands on the king's crimson beard and kissed his cheeks. They flashed small, knowing smiles at their mother then bade their father farewell and quickly left the room.

King Edward looked fixedly at Queen Philippa. Something unspoken passed between them. Perhaps the queen's point had been made. There were innocent children in Calais—children like his daughters, Isabella and Joan. Children like Abigail and Daniel.

Suddenly, Abigail understood why the queen had dressed her up. Queen Philippa needed to put a face to the children of Calais.

"Bring in a scribe, Edward," the king said to his son.

Daniel used the distraction to motion Abigail over to the table. The queen had taken her seat again by the fireplace, so Abigail inched over to him.

"What is going on? What have you done?" he asked quietly, looking her up and down.

"You think this is my doing?" she said, looking down at her dress.

"Well, is it?" he snapped.

Abigail sighed. "Yes. I convinced the queen that she should take me aside and treat me to the finest English clothes and food. I threw myself at her feet and begged until she relented. I made quite a scene. Crying. Begging. You name it!"

"Wait," Daniel interrupted. "You had food?"

"I drank something from a royal goblet, yes."

Daniel clenched his teeth.

She smiled. She couldn't help it. He was overreacting, wasn't he? There was no way two teens were going to change history.

Prince Edward returned with a dark-haired man in fine clothes who looked like his thin mustache had been painted with two delicate strokes of an artist's brush. He unrolled a length of leather and pulled out a piece of parchment, a pen, and an inkwell. The scribe arranged everything carefully, then held his pen at the ready.

The king cleared his throat. "Governor Jean de Vienne. On this day, the 3rd of August, the year of our Lord 1347, I hereby..." The king paused and looked over at Abigail and Daniel, then at the queen.

The queen hurried over and quickly ushered them out of the room. With the door safely shut behind them, the queen spoke to them in a whisper. "I've done what I can. Farewell."

And just like that, the queen strolled down the hall and disappeared into her room.

Within minutes, a new letter with the king's seal was placed in Daniel's hand and they were marched back through the English camp to the gate of Calais. As the gate reopened and the drawbridge lowered, Abigail asked Daniel the burning question.

"What happens now?"

"Let's hope it's what is supposed to happen," Daniel replied, giving her dress another look.

"Does King Edward pardon the town?" she asked, ignoring his cold remark.

"Yes, with stipulations."

"What are stipulations?" This word she didn't know, and she was anxious to add it to her word vault.

"Conditions," Daniel said.

"What kind of conditions?" Abigail's stomach churned. Suddenly, the thrill of meeting the queen had vanished and fear crept in.

Before she could ask Daniel more, they were across the bridge where Governor de Vienne was waiting for them. Daniel handed him the king's letter. Jean ripped open the seal and read, his lips moving silently. What little color he had left in his face drained away.

"Did he give the town a pardon?" Abigail asked. "The queen—"

The governor cut her off. "Come. I must call a town meeting immediately."

Abigail's throat tightened. By the look on his face, the news did not appear to be good.

Not good at all.

# CHAPTER
# TEN

*Calais, France*
*August 3, 1347*
*Jean de Fiennes – with Pierre de Wissant*

J ean sat at the table and stared at the hearth in the
middle of the floor. The room grew darker as a cloud
passed over the smoke hole in the vaulted roof. A small
mouse was nibbling at the rushes covering the floor.
There were no crumbs to be found. It'd been one hundred days
since food had been smuggled into the city.

Jean regretted turning down Pierre's invitation to lunch. He
poked his fingers between his ribs. There were twenty-four
ribs, or twelve pairs. He fought the urge to count them again,
then considered whether he should try to catch the mouse and
roast it. But as he stared at the tiny creature, he found himself
feeling sorry for it. Rats were easier to stomach. They were ugly

and greedy. A mouse only searched for the tiniest of morsels to quell its hunger just like Jean did.

A bell tolled in the distance. Three rings and a pause—three rings and a pause. Word must have come back from King Edward. The bell was a call to the town hall for the prominent burghers of Calais. His father would have been counted among those to answer the call were he still alive. He had been the town's most prominent wine merchant. The store at the front of the house stood empty now—closed. The barrels of wine in the storage cellar underneath the house had sold out months ago. Jean was all alone now in a house too large for one person. Orphaned at eighteen, he wondered what kind of future he'd have?

A loud bang on the door came from the front of the house. He considered ignoring it. Many desperate people had come knocking, thinking a rich merchant may have food or drink to share. Though now that the poorest had been let out of the city because there was no food to give them, there had been no visitors of late.

"Jean!" a muffled voice cried.

More banging came.

He stood and shuffled down the hall. He avoided looking into the room on the left—the storefront. He half feared seeing the ghost of his father.

"Jean!"

The front door rattled fiercely beneath someone's pounding fists.

Jean opened the door to find Pierre. Seeing him there now, shallow-faced and thin, Jean recalled better times when he'd let Pierre in to see his father.

Pierre and his brother Jacques had been friends of Jean's father and had grown the grapes required for his wine making on their fine estates outside of Calais. Who knew what had become of their land now? He had heard that the English pillaged the countryside at night, taking what wasn't theirs.

"Come. They're calling us to town hall," Pierre said.

"Why would I go?" Jean asked.

Pierre removed his hat and scratched his head. "You stand in for your father now."

Jean shook his head. "No one wants to hear my opinion." Truth be told, he felt too weak to walk the short journey to town hall.

He tried to close the door, but Pierre stopped it with his hand. He was surprisingly strong for someone who was so malnourished.

"He would want you to stand up for his good name," Pierre said, more forcefully this time.

"Would he?"

"A good son brings honor to his father."

Something about the intensity of Pierre's eyes broke through Jean's defenses. He fought the urge to cry. Instead, he nodded and grabbed his felt cap off a peg by the door.

CHAPTER

# ELEVEN

T he wealthiest citizens of Calais poured into town
hall. There was an eerie silence to their gathering, as
if the meeting were a funeral. Abigail and Daniel
stood back against the plaster wall near the door. The guard
assigned to watch them leaned into the wall with slumped
shoulders, seeming to have lost interest in his duty. Governor
Jean de Vienne stood at the front, waiting. Something in his
eyes made him look lost.

Just as a solider was about to close the door, two late
arrivals slipped in and the doors were closed with a sickening
thud. The room was full, so the two men stayed by the door
and removed their hats. The younger man standing next to
Abigail pushed his wavy brown hair out of his face and glanced
over at her, nodding as a way of polite greeting. He wore a
simple brown tunic belted at the waist and black pants
haphazardly stuffed into his soft boots.

The young man then turned and spoke softly to the older
man next to him. "Pierre—"

"You should be here, Jean. Don't worry," the man said.

*Pierre. Jean.*

Abigail swallowed. These were real people with real lives. Had she and Daniel made it worse for them with King Edward or better?

She wiped her sweaty hands on her fine dress. Suddenly she wished she were still wearing the grain sack.

"We have received word from King Edward," the governor said. "Our terms of surrender have been denied and new conditional terms have been given."

The men in the room looked to each other in worried confusion as the women pulled their children close to them.

"King Edward will pardon the people of Calais if we surrender the keys of the city and if six of our chief burghers surrender themselves to him to be punished as he sees fit."

The room erupted with wails and shouting.

"He intends to kill them!"

"We'd rather starve!"

Abigail turned to Daniel and grabbed his arm. "Did we do this?"

Daniel pulled his arm from her grasp. "So far, so good. This was what really happened in history."

"How is this good?" she whispered fiercely. "People are going to die."

A voice boomed above the chaos. "Sirs!"

The room quickly quieted as a man with shoulder-length silvery hair and a matching beard strolled slowly to the front of the room. He was wearing a long, belted, navy tunic that came to his ankles. A gray cloak was draped across one shoulder with a silver clasp. It was clear by the quiet attention of the people that the man was well-respected.

The governor placed a hand on the man's shoulder. "The governor recognizes Eustache de Saint Pierre."

Eustache thanked the governor then stood facing the

people. His clothes, though fine, hung on this frail frame. He scanned the room with his deep brown eyes waiting until he had everyone's full attention.

"It would be a pity for so many to die of hunger if we can prevent it," he said. "I have lived a rich and full life. I have had more wealth and riches than most. But my conscience now demands that I must do what is right. That is why I offer myself as the first of the six to take King Edward's punishment for Calais."

Several men and women ran forward and fell at Eustache's feet. Tears streamed down their faces. Eustache lips quivered, but he did not cry.

Abigail covered her mouth with her hands, stifling a sob.

*This is what bravery looks like.*

The younger man, Jean, shuffled nervously next to her. She wanted to tell him it would be okay, but she didn't know if it would be.

*When have I ever had to worry about an army camped outside my city or where my next meal was going to come from?*

Suddenly, her angst about turning thirteen seemed ridiculous.

Another man, dressed in a burgundy tunic and pants, came to the front of the room and stood next to Eustache. "I will be the second and go with my friend, Eustache."

The governor, full of emotion with tears falling from his eyes, said, "Jean d'Aire, your city thanks you."

Two fair-haired young women wept loudly and held each other. The man was clearly their father.

Another man stepped forward. "I will be the third."

"Jacques de Wissant," the governor said, "your city thanks you."

Abigail watched as the older man by the door, Pierre, bowed his head and rubbed a hand over his head. The young man, Jean, grabbed his friend's arm. "Pierre! Your brother!"

Pierre quietly pulled free from Jean's arm and left him, joining the other men at the front of the room.

Abigail's heart sank.

"I, Pierre de Wissant, will be the fourth!" He fiercely embraced his brother, Jacques. The governor thanked him. The women and children belonging to these brave men huddled together, consoling each other, weeping in each other's arms.

Jean fidgeted with his hat, griping it tightly in his hands. He was clearly distressed that his friend had volunteered.

Another man stepped forward. "I, Adrieu d'Andres will be fifth."

It was quiet for a time after that except for the soft sobs and whimpers of the families of the five men. No one else came forward. They needed a sixth volunteer.

"I should volunteer," Jean said softly next to Abigail. He turned to her, looking for something. *Courage?* She wasn't sure what to do, but she didn't want Jean to die.

"You don't have to do this," she said, hoping he could understand English. "You're young. You have your whole life ahead of you."

"No," he said, looking down while shaking his head. "Not anymore. Both of my parents, the de Fiennes, are dead."

Abigail looked over at Daniel. He shook his head solemnly. Her stomach dropped. *Jean volunteers? I can't stop him, or I'll change history.* She turned back and did the only thing she could think to do.

"Jean," she said, looking him in the eyes, "if you do this, you will be remembered, forever. I promise I'll never forget you."

He smiled weakly. "What's your name?" he asked.

"Abigail."

He took her hand and kissed the top of it like a valiant knight. "Thank you, Abigail. I'll take the memory of your kindness with me."

He gave her his hat and went to the front of the room.

"I, Jean de Fiennes, will be the sixth!"

The other five volunteers embraced Jean. Tears flooded Abigail's eyes as Jean's hat warmed her hands. She turned to Daniel and fell into his arms.

"I want to go home, Daniel."

But Daniel didn't say anything; he just told her it would be okay. But nothing was okay.

Nothing.

# CHAPTER

# TWELVE

Abigail and Daniel stood with the citizens of Calais outside the town hall. The six men who had volunteered their lives to save the city filed out into the street. All of their fine clothing was gone. Each man wore nothing except a long white shirt. They wore no cap or shoes. They were to present themselves to King Edward stripped of their dignity. Nooses made from thick rope were placed around their necks—another condition of the king.

The townspeople cried silently as a procession began behind the men, and they all moved as one toward the city gate. Abigail and Daniel walked in front. They would go with the men and be returned to their king. She wished she could have explained that Edward was not her king, that she hated what he was doing to Calais, but those words would have been lost among the suffering.

The mass of people walked slowly and silently. When the iron gate lifted and the drawbridge lowered, the families of the doomed men rushed forward, and clung to their loved ones.

Finally, some of the soldiers had to separate them so the men could leave.

No one came to say good-bye to the youngest volunteer, Jean de Fiennes. He had no one to mourn his loss. Abigail's eyes met his, and they held each other's gaze.

*I'll never forgot you, Jean. I promise.*

The governor handed her the keys to the city and told her to give them to her king. The truth of these men's situations reflected in the governor's watery eyes. The burghers of Calais would never return home, and she wondered silently if she ever would either. But she could hardly think of that now. Not in the midst of such tragedy.

The walk across the bridge felt like the longest walk she'd ever taken. England's Prince Edward and a dozen other soldiers mounted on horses were waiting for them on the other side of the moat. She closed her eyes and clenched her teeth as the gate clanged shut behind them. King Edward's whole camp was waiting this time. There was no busy market like before. The king's men were not going about their business. They were watching and waiting. Even the workers and laborers had stopped and put their work aside. Many removed their hats in respect, knowing the fate of the men of Calais was grim.

She had expected that the burghers of Calais would be spat upon or yelled at, but there was none of that. Had the shock of seeing how thin and gaunt the men were stilled the enemy's tongues?

They passed through the camp and crowds silently until they reached King Edward's grand living quarters. A platform had been set up in front of the wooden palace, and King Edward sat upon a wooden throne in the attendance of two soldiers dressed in mail armor and helmets. A short, stocky man in a long, tailored jacket stood by the king. Abigail

searched for Queen Philippa, but it was hardly the proper place
or setting for a pregnant woman.

Daniel grabbed Abigail by the arm. "Where's the queen?"
he whispered fiercely.

"What do you mean? Is she supposed to be here?"

"Yes!"

One of the king's armored soldiers approached and took the
keys to the city from Abigail, and then motioned the men of
Calais to climb the steps to the platform. Before she could get
more details from Daniel, the first man to volunteer in Calais, and
the most senior, Eustache de Saint Pierre, knelt before the king.
The other five knelt behind him in unison and bowed their heads.

"Most Honorable King," Eustache said in English. "We
have come freely, yielding ourselves to you in order to save the
citizens of Calais, who have suffered much pain and distress.
But we ask for your mercy, that you will spare us as well." He
bowed his head and waited.

The noble-looking man next to the king leaned down and
whispered into the king's ear. The king stood and furrowed his
brow, looking out across the crowd.

"I will do as I please!" he shouted.

The English people crowded around the scene shouted,
"Off with their heads," but a few voices cried for mercy. She
couldn't believe it. Some of the king's people were coming to
the defense of their enemy! The man who stood by the king
engaged him in a heated discussion. Was he trying to talk the
king into sparing the men?

"Who is that?" Abigail asked Daniel.

"If I had to guess, I'd say it was Sir Walter Manny, admiral
of the English Navy."

"Maybe he'll talk some sense into the king?" she asked
hopefully.

"No. He won't," Daniel said searching the crowd. "Look, we have a problem. A *big* problem."

"What could be worse than this?" she asked.

King Edward raised a hand, hushing the crowd. "Bring the headsman!"

The crowd shouted insults mixed with shouts of mercy. A red-faced Sir Manny snapped his fingers and a solider left to fetch the executioner.

"I'll tell you what is worse," Daniel said. "How about all six of these men being beheaded in front of us."

Abigail shook her head. "I don't understand. Isn't that the point? The men die to save their city?"

Daniel shook his head. "The queen saves them, Abigail. She talks the king out of killing them. Or she's supposed to, anyway."

Her mouth fell open.

"We have to do something," she said frantically. The crowd began to part to the right of them.

"The executioner is coming. Any brilliant ideas?" Daniel asked, looking grim.

The cries for justice grew louder. The king stood on his platform looking smug. The men of Calais were forced to turn and face the crowd, still on their knees. Their bodies shook with fear.

Young Jean peered over at her. His eyes were glassy with tears. That was all it took to spur her on.

"Come on," she said, grabbing at Daniel's wrist. "We're going to find the queen!"

She shoved her way through the crowd, going behind the king's platform. Daniel stayed right on her heels. The wooden castle had been left with one lone guard by the huge carved doors. Abigail wasted no time. She marched right up to the only thing standing between her and the salvation of the men of Calais.

"We need to see the queen immediately!" she announced.

The guard looked them up and down—she in her fine dress, and Daniel in his 1800s clothes and cap. The soldier crossed his arms. "The queen is...indisposed," he said with an amused smirk.

Abigail looked over at Daniel. "What does 'indisposed' mean?" she asked.

"It means she's not available. She's busy."

Abigail hastily stored the word away.

Daniel raised an eyebrow and motioned ever so slightly toward the guard. "Wake snakes," he whispered.

The crowd's shouts of "Off with their heads," were echoing behind them.

She nodded.

The guard narrowed his eyes. But before the man could uncross his arms, Daniel leaped forward and drew the guard's sword from its scabbard, then backed away, wielding its sharp tip.

The man lunged toward Daniel. "Give me that, you little churl!"

"Come and get it, you old back of a goat's behind!" Daniel grinned then ran off with the guard on his heels.

Daniel may have had a weird vocabulary, but Abigail couldn't help but think how his words perfectly fit the moment. She smiled and shook her head in amazement as Daniel dropped to his knees and crawled, sword in hand, through the legs of the thick crowd. The guard pushed and shoved his way through, like a bull in a china shop. *Ooo, metaphor.* She gave herself a mental pat on the back and hurried inside the castle.

She took off running down the hall toward the queen's room.

*We can still save the men of Calais. There's still time!*

She was filled with such joy and hope until her foot struck something and...

*Thud!*

She fell face first on the hall rug, her chin stinging from the impact.

*What happened?*

She pushed herself to her knees, and there stood Edward the Black blocking her way to the queen.

# CHAPTER
# THIRTEEN

The handsome son of the king casually pulled back the leg he had tripped her with. True to his name, he was still dressed in all black—the fabric of his tunic finely embroidered with the English lion crest.

He laughed at her. "What's the rush?"

Heat rose to her face. She balled her hands into fists. "You know what the hurry is," she said between clenched teeth.

He smirked. "What? Those knaves outside? They deserve what they're going to get. Calais should have surrendered when we asked them to."

She stored the word knave to look up later. But she was beginning to wonder if there would be a later for her. Abigail rose to her feet and tried to move past the prince, but he matched her movements, blocking every attempt.

*I'm running out of time.*

So, she did what girls do best. She screamed at the top of her lungs.

Edward's eyes widened, and he took a step back. He may have been a knight, but she was betting he knew nothing of how to handle a raging, screaming female. She continued screaming, mustering every fiber of breath left in her lungs until she was empty of air.

The doors to the queen's room flung open. Queen Philippa stepped into the hall, holding a hand to her baby bump. "What's the meaning of this...?"

Edward turned to her and held up a hand. "It's nothing mother, go back to your room."

"It's not nothing!" Abigail blurted out. She stepped around Edward.

The queen looked surprised to see her.

"Your Majesty, the king has ordered the beheading of six burghers of Calais. They've asked for mercy, but the king has denied their request and sent for the executioner."

The queen looked to her son. "Did you know about this?"

Edward took a deep breath and shrugged. "The king does what the king does."

Abigail rushed past young Edward and dared to take the queen by the hand. "Please, Your Majesty, please help these men."

She nodded. "Lead the way."

As they passed Edward, Queen Philippa paused briefly and spoke to him under her breath. "You and I will talk later."

Edward's face reddened with embarrassment.

*How did I ever think he was handsome and charming?* Abigail resisted sticking her tongue out at him and hitting him with a *Who's a big, bad knight now?*

The queen moved slower than Abigail would have liked.

"I should have seen this coming," the queen said. "But I'm afraid our earlier encounter tired me out more than I realized. I must have fallen asleep."

Abigail's throat swelled like she'd swallowed a bag of rocks.

*So, it's my fault the queen wasn't where she was supposed to be. If those men die, it will be because of me.*

"We should hurry," Abigail said taking Queen Philippa's arm. Formalities seemed pointless at the moment, and she prayed the queen wouldn't interpret her boldness as anything but concern.

Outside, the guard was still missing and there was no sign of Daniel. She had to give Daniel credit. He was clever when he needed to be.

The crowd had swelled and completely surrounded the platform.

Abigail yelled out, "Make way for the queen," and the crowd immediately parted in a wave of bows.

When they reached the platform, Abigail's mouth fell open. The six men of Calais were still on the platform, facing the crowd on their knees, but the ropes had been removed from their necks and white blindfolds had been tied over their eyes. Every one of them held their hands together in prayer, their lips moving silently, their bodies trembling.

The executioner stood above them, pacing from one end of the platform to the other, wielding his thick sword. He was not what she would have imagined. The man wasn't big and bare-chested like the movies. He was average size, though his arms looked bigger than most. There was no black hood or large ax. He had on blue tights, a gray tunic, and a cap, like he was attending a fancy picnic. Boy, did history have the whole big, bad executioner man in a leather mask with a giant ax thing wrong.

The executioner stepped up to Eustache and looked to the king who was once again sitting on this wooden throne.

King Edward templed his fingers and nodded.

The executioner raised his sword.

Many in the crowd cheered him on, but others were watching in despair.

Upon seeing this display, the queen wasted no time.

"STOP!" she cried out.

Daniel appeared abruptly at Abigail's side, out of breath, but otherwise intact and sword free. Together they helped the queen up the steps of the platform.

The executioner looked once again to the king. The king waved him off Eustache, then rose and greeted his wife.

"My Queen," he said taking her hand. "You shouldn't be here. It's not good for your condition."

Philippa reclaimed her hand. "On the contrary. This is exactly where I should be."

To the amazement of all, she lowered herself to her knees with great difficulty. Abigail took a step forward, but Daniel put out a hand to stop her.

*Don't throw a pebble into history.*

This was their only chance to make things right.

"What are you doing?" the king said gently.

Queen Philippa stared up into the king's eyes. "I've come across the sea and with much danger to see you. I've asked nothing of you since my arrival. But now I beg you, if you love me and our unborn child, you'll show mercy to these men." She bowed her head before her husband and her king as a servant would.

The crowd became eerily quiet. King Edward looked across the crowd of people then back down at his wife.

Abigail held her breath.

The king went to one knee and lifted the queen's chin with his hand. Tears streamed down the queen's face.

King Edward was quiet, but only for a moment.

"How can I refuse you when you come to me in this way?"

He placed his hand on her stomach and she covered his hand with hers.

"I give these men to you to do as you please," he said. He stood and faced the crowd. "Calais must surrender their land, but I will spare their lives!"

The crowd erupted with cheers as the king helped the queen to her feet. She brought the king's ringed hand to her lips and kissed it, then immediately called for the king's soldiers to remove the blindfolds from the men. The six burghers of Calais held their hands to the sky in gratitude and embraced each other in relief.

Abigail and Daniel gave each other a quick hug with huge grins on their faces. History had remained intact and the brave men of Calais and their fellow townspeople had been spared.

The queen called attendants to find clothes for the men and to immediately prepare a large feast.

"We have to go," Daniel said.

Abigail was so caught up in the moment, she barely heard him. "What?" she asked absently.

Young Jean de Fienne looked her way. He put both of his hands over his heart and bowed in her direction.

*He's going to live! But people will still remember him forever because of Rodin's sculptures.*

Daniel took her by the arm and tugged a little. She turned to him, ready to give him a piece of her mind. But the seriousness of his expression stopped her.

"Now's our chance to return to Calais and go home," he said. "We need to leave. Now."

*Home.*

She'd almost forgotten. In a strange way, Calais had started to feel like home—like she belonged there. But this wasn't her home.

She nodded, taking one final look back at Jean de Fienne.

70

He smiled weakly and raised a hand in farewell just as a fine cloak was placed over his shoulders. He seemed to sense he was never going to see her again. She waved back and willed herself not to cry. Daniel took her hand, and they ran through the English camp back to Calais.

# FOURTEEN

They delivered the good news to the Governor of Calais that the men had been spared. A spark lit in his eyes, and he wasted no time in summoning men to ring the town's bell. Abigail and Daniel were left alone. Free. Free to go home.

Once they were at the top of the watchtower, Abigail touched Daniel's arm to stop him from saying the portal password. She needed a moment to look across the water at King Edward's camp and the ships in the harbor. She never wanted to forget what she'd witnessed here. She took a deep breath of sea air then looked over at Daniel and nodded. He took her hand.

"Through me is the way into the doleful city," he said with a hint of sadness.

Her heart sank. For it was sad to leave a place full of life that had long ago been extinguished by time.

Abigail was hit with a blinding light and the feeling of falling. She fell into swirling light and darkness and warm air that smelled of seaweed and sand. Then, in the blink of an eye, she was staring at the gravel beneath her feet and breathing in the welcoming aroma of grass and leaves. They were right where they had been when the morning had started—in Rodin's garden in front of his sculpture, *The Three Shades*. She was home.

Her scarf was back around her neck and her bag was draped across her shoulder, even though she had ditched both in Calais as they'd run to escape from the woman in black. The dress the queen had dressed her in had been replaced with her jeans and T-shirt. She wiggled her toes inside her shoes, just to make sure they were all there. She touched her frizzy hair. The fancy weave was gone.

"Everything you take with you comes back," Daniel said, sounding worried.

Was he expecting her to be angry? She was anything but angry. "That was..." She turned in a circle taking in everything around her—Rodin's sculptures, the blue sky, the Raleigh air. "It was..." She searched for the right words.

"I'm sorry," Daniel blurted out. "I was wrong to take you through a time portal. I ruined your birthday—"

She reached out and put her finger on his lips just long enough to quiet him. His eyes widened.

"Daniel. That was the most awesome birthday *EVER!*"

Daniel grinned, and his eyes sparkled. "Told you I had a surprise for you."

Abigail frowned, and his smile disappeared.

"But," she added.

"Uh-oh," Daniel said, losing the smile.

"You have *a lot* of explaining to do."

He removed his cap. "I know."

Just then, a strange feeling came over her—like someone was watching her.

She turned and faced the reflecting pond. The men of

Rodin's sculptures that surrounded the pond were identical to the *real* burghers of Calais!

She wandered toward the statue of the man with long hair and a beard. He stood slightly slumped, as if he were having difficulty moving forward. She stood in front of him and gazed into the hollow eyes of Eustache de Saint Pierre—the first man in Calais who had volunteered his life to save the city.

Daniel approached silently by her side.

"How is this possible?" she asked. "It looks just like Eustache. Rodin couldn't have possibly known what he looked like."

"I know," he said. "The resemblance is uncanny."

"Uncanny?" she asked, not knowing the meaning of the word.

"Extraordinary," he said.

"Yes," she said, studying the rope around Eustache's neck. "Extraordinary."

Then it hit her. *Jean.*

*Jean de Fiennes. The young volunteer—the one she promised that he would never be forgotten.*

Was he there as well?

She whipped around, her heart pounding.

Daniel pointed just past Eustache.

She ran to the statue and froze. It was him. It was Jean de Fiennes from head to toe—the wavy hair, the high cheek bones. And even though the eyes of the statue were hollow, she would never forget the intensity of his gaze.

*I wonder if he remembered me.*

Daniel broke the silence. "Do you think it's possible...?"

"What?" she asked, looking over at him.

He swallowed. "That Rodin..."

"Are you suggesting Rodin...*time traveled*?"

Daniel spun around. "How else would you explain all of

this? When Rodin was commissioned by Calais to create a monument to the bravery of the men of Calais, he came back with these. Sorrowful, fearful men. Men filled with anguish."

"He sculpted them how they really were," she said. "Brave, weak, and afraid."

Daniel nodded. "The Calais committee wasn't happy with Rodin. They wanted valiant, strong looking men."

"He captured what he saw," she said, not believing it possible that Rodin could have time traveled just like she and Daniel had.

"Rodin portrayed the human emotion of the men, something real," Daniel said.

She turned in a slow circle taking in all the men she'd come to know. "This is amazing."

"Thank you," Daniel suddenly said.

"For what?"

"I don't know," he said. "For being my friend."

He said it in a sad kind of way, and she realized there was much more to his story than she knew. Much more.

"You can trust me, you know," she said.

"I know," he said, offering her a weak smile. "I'm not sure where to start."

She placed a hand on his shoulder. "Just start at the beginning."

# PART TWO

DANIEL

...SECURE COMM TRANSMISSION TO THE
FANTASTIC ORDER OF ODD TRAVELERS
FROM TRAVELER #2520

...PORTAL ACTIVITY CONFIRMED

...TARGET STATUS: IN PURSUIT

...10:20:00 INTERSTELLAR TIME

# CHAPTER
# FIFTEEN

Daniel and Abigail sat outside under the birch trees at one of the small bistro tables next to the museum's East Building. Though they had spent all day in Calais, no time had passed in the present. The morning sun was still slowly rising to its afternoon peak. Daniel had all day to explain the unexplainable.

"I'm not from this time," he said. "And, clearly, my mother does not work at the museum."

He studied Abigail's face, noting a slight movement in her left eyebrow. Subtle skepticism? He was good at reading people.

*She doesn't believe me.*

"That actually makes sense," Abigail said.

He couldn't keep his mouth from falling open with what he was inwardly feeling—shock.

*So much for being good at reading people.*

Presuming that he'd mistaken her reaction, (because, after all, time travel was impossible as anyone knew) he stood and paced in front of her. Her singular enchanting smile almost derailed his thoughts.

"You don't think I'm off my chump?" he asked, gesturing wildly.

"My chump?"

He ran his hand through his hair then tapped the dimple on his chin looking for the right word.

"Unsound mind," he said. "You don't think I'm of unsound mind?"

Abigail appeared to stifle a laugh. "Well, let's worry about your mind later." She stood and placed her hands on his shoulders. "You talk different. You dress different. You act different." She dropped her arms to her side and sighed. "It's clear that you're not from this time."

He cocked his head, puzzled. "Really? I thought I was fitting in quite nicely."

"It wasn't meant to be an insult," she said. "It's charming, in an 1800s sort of way."

He rubbed the back of his neck. "Yes. 1800s seems right. I mean my clothes kind of look like the ones the kids are wearing in the painting *The Tough Story* hanging in the American gallery."

Abigail studied his attire. "Maybe a bit more formal than that."

He nodded. His clothes were a little finer, though well-worn and a bit threadbare.

Abigail plopped down into her seat. "Now that we've established *when* you're likely from, let me hear the rest."

He sat down rather gingerly on the edge of his seat and spilled out everything he knew in less than thirty seconds.

All he could remember was his first name and that he'd somehow traveled forward in time from the 1800s with nothing more than the clothes on his back and the small red book. In that book were pages of art which were identified as time travel portals, though there was no indication of where the portals led. In the back of the book was a list of cities, each with a designated return portal. Those return portals appeared to be places that still existed in the current time. He didn't know why he had the book, where he'd gotten it, or why he'd used it in the first place. He had no recollection of his last name or his parents—if he had parents. He could be an orphan for all he knew.

"Wow," Abigail said when he'd finished. She looked at him askance. "So, you've been trying different portals, looking for your way back home because the book doesn't say where the portals lead."

He nodded then pulled the book out of his pants pocket and set it on the table.

"And the only way you've managed to get back to the museum is because there's a list of places with return portals in the back of the book. Like 'Calais, France—watchtower'."

He nodded again. It sounded even crazier when someone said it out loud.

Abigail picked up the red book and flipped through it. Her eyes widened as she scanned page after page. "There must be fifty or more pieces of artwork listed in here."

"They don't all work."

She shut the book. "How many have you tried?"

"I don't know. Ten."

"Ten!"

"Only two have worked."

The middle-aged couple sitting nearby glanced over at them. Daniel grabbed the book and stuffed it back into his pocket. The couple gathered their things and walked toward the parking lot.

"So Rodin..." Abigail said.

"First time trying that portal. Clearly not the way home. Before Calais, I'd only found one portal that worked. The *Man Scraping Chocolate* painting sent me to Spain."

Abigail studied his face.

"I didn't want to drag you into whatever this is, but I really need a friend," he added.

"Well, I know you've been here at least a week. Where have you been staying all this time?"

"The woods, or an empty metal thing with wheels if it's raining."

"You mean an empty car?"

He shrugged.

"Daniel, I'm so sorry. You should have told me sooner."

He laughed a little. "When we met last weekend, you looked at me like I was a two-headed toad. I think 'Hi, I've come here from the past and I need help getting back,' wouldn't have exactly earned your trust."

She smiled. "Yeah. You're probably right."

"If only I could remember where I came from, or why, it might help us figure out how to get me back, but I can't remember anything!"

"What portal got you here?" she asked. "This museum didn't exist in the 1800s."

Daniel sighed. "I don't remember."

Abigail shook her head and stood up.

*Is she going to leave?*

His heart raced.

"There's only one thing to do," she announced.

A lump formed in Daniel's throat. She was all he had. If he lost her...

"We keep trying portals until you find your way home," she said.

"We?" he asked, standing. "You mean, you'll go with me even after...Calais?"

She smiled and nodded.

He jumped up and threw his arms around her. Abigail laughed a little. She'd given him hope for the first time since he'd arrived. When he realized he was squeezing her too hard, he abruptly backed away.

"Sorry," he said, his face flushing.

"It's okay," she said. "What are friends for?"

"You consider me a friend?" he asked quietly, almost whispering it.

She rolled her eyes, but her wry smile told him everything he needed to know. His friend was going to help him get back home.

"Okay, let's see this book of yours," Abigail said, holding out her hand.

Daniel gave her the red book, and they sat back down. He tapped his fingers on the table while she flipped through it.

"What about *A Meat Stall with the Holy Family Giving Alms* by Pieter Aertsen?" She glanced over at him.

"Tried it. Doesn't work."

She turned to the next page. "*Aphrodite-Isis,* artist unknown?"

"Cold as a wagon wheel."

She sighed and glared at him.

"Sorry. Means the portal is dead. Doesn't work."

He took the book from her, opened it up to a random page, closed his eyes, and stabbed a finger onto the page.

He opened one eye to see where his finger landed. "*The Finding of Moses* by Luca Giordano." He displayed a wide smile. But Abigail only crossed her arms and frowned.

"This is how you're going to decide what portal to try?" she asked. "That's not much of a plan."

He shrugged. "One portal is as good as another. I told you, the book doesn't say where they go. Any of them could be my way home."

"I'd feel better if we had some kind of a plan."

"What if the *plan* is to not have a plan?" he asked, raising an eyebrow. "It's not like we have control over where we go next."

She narrowed her eyes. "Fine," she said, unfolding her arms.

Satisfied, he quickly memorized the password. It was better to have it committed to memory in case a quick return was necessary. When he looked up, Abigail had already taken off toward the West Building where the Italian collection was housed. "Uh, Abigail," he said, racing after her. But she was clearly a girl on a mission. She'd disappeared inside the museum before he could catch up.

Breathless, Daniel found Abigail in front of the large painting by the Italian artist. She was taking it in as if she were inhaling its entirety. Several women in the painting were gathered at the edges of the Nile river, and were staring down at baby Moses. The ladies had a subtle brilliance to them, as if they had been illuminated by the presence of something divine.

"The princess doesn't look Egyptian," Abigail suddenly said. "Isn't she supposed to be the Pharaoh's daughter?"

The painting had a regal nature to it that screamed castles and kingdoms, not ancient Egypt and the reedy banks of the Nile. The Pharaoh's daughter in this painting was queen-like— a pale woman in a golden gown with a blue cloak trimmed in white fur draped across her shoulders. She stared down at the equally pale baby figure of Moses floating in a basket.

"Modern interpretation of the times?" Daniel suggested.

That seemed to satisfy Abigail, and her next look was one of expectation. "You don't have to do this," he said.

"Yes, I do."

They turned and faced the painting, waiting until they were both certain that no one was nearby or looking their way. Daniel reached out his hand and her slender fingers slid into his. He spoke the password, hoping this portal would work and that maybe this time it would be his way home.

*"May we find the favor of him who dwelt in the burning bush."*

A flash of light. The museum faded. Sound dissolved. He melted into darkness and fell into nothingness. The first thing Daniel sensed before his vision cleared was a waft of sweltering heat and the distinct smell of animal poo.

# CHAPTER
# SIXTEEN

*Thebes, Egypt*
*609 BC*
*MeryPath*

"MeryPath! Must you stop for every animal?"

Her mother was using the long version of her name. That wasn't a good sign.

Mery shoved her leather sandals under one armpit and quickly knelt in the warm sand. She motioned for the small, brown monkey to come take the fig that she held in her open palm. It was flood season and the Nile had spilled over its banks, forcing the monkeys that lived along its edges to seek drier land.

*How marvelous it would be to live on the Nile among the palm trees.*

"Quit feeding the monkeys and come along. They can fend for themselves."

Mery had always wanted a monkey for a pet, but her mother had said they had a perfectly fine cat and that would have to do. The monkey seemed to sense that the window of opportunity was closing and quickly snatched the treat from her hand and clambered away. Mery reluctantly joined her mother, who immediately resumed her speedy walk toward the temple of Amun—the king of all gods in Thebes.

Unlike other gods, Amun was everywhere and unseen, like the wind. She liked that. Her mother, Djedmut, prayed more often to Nut—the mother-goddess. Nut swallowed the sun every night and birthed it the next morning. Perhaps that was why her mother liked the sun goddess best. The sun was something you could depend on. Djedmut liked order and certainty. Mery would rather race with the wind and be whisked away by the sky, unseen.

"What's the hurry?" Mery asked. But she had a pretty good idea that her mother was going to the temple to speak with Mery's father.

That morning someone had delivered a very fine papyrus scroll sealed with a wax scarab to their home. That in itself was not unusual. Her father, Jahi, was a priest, and he often received important documents. But the message hadn't been for her father; it had been for her mother, Djedmut. Mery had tried to read over her mother's shoulder, but Djedmut quickly turned away, keeping Mery from reading it. The only thing she'd caught a glimpse of was the Pharaoh's name, Necho II.

What could the Pharaoh possibly have to say to her mother? The Pharaoh's home was far north in Zau. They were located south in Thebes. She was about to ask about the scroll when her mother spoke.

"Mery, you must continue to keep up your reading and writing while I'm gone. Practice every day."

Mery's heart beat a little faster. Her mother had never left her, not once.

"Where are you going?" Mery asked. The beginnings of worry seeped into her ka, the center of her spirit, and she quickly said a prayer to Shu, the god of peace, for calm.

Djedmut ignored Mery's question.

"You must keep your writing from your father," she said.

"I don't understand why we keep it from him. Wouldn't he be proud of me? No other girls I know can read and write."

Her mother stopped and glared at her. Mery absently rubbed her feet across the sand.

"You know a woman can't be trained formally as a scribe unless she is a priestess."

"Yet, you are a scribe," Mery said. "Surely the goddess of writing herself, Seshat, has guided your path."

Her mother smiled weakly. "My father had no son to pass on his knowledge as a scribe. He trained me, yes, but no one accepts me as a real scribe. You know this, Mery. I teach you because I have no son. I must pass on my father's legacy or it will die with me."

"But if Father sees how good I am at it..."

Djedmut shook her head sadly. "He hates that I scribe for the farmers after the harvest and translate for the foreigners who have settled here. I'm sorry, Mery. For now, your reading and writing must stay between us."

Mery looked into her mother's dark eyes. She'd always thought her mother beautiful. Djedmut's long hair hung like strands of black silk around her shoulders. The black kohl she wore under her eyes made them sparkle in the desert sun. Though she had on a simple white shift, the alabaster at her neck and the gold bracelets on her wrists showed that she was favored among the gods.

Mery nodded, submitting to her mother, but silently she

touched the amulet of Seshat that hung around her neck and prayed that the goddess would allow Mery to become a scribe like her mother, even if it was only for merchants and farmers.

"Come, we must hurry," Djedmut said.

Mery still had no idea why the Pharaoh had called upon her mother or where she was going, but Mery had already decided that she wasn't going to be left behind.

# CHAPTER
# SEVENTEEN

"Snakes alive! What is that foul smell?" Daniel gasped, fanning the hot air. Surrounding them on all sides was a city of buildings that looked like giant sandcastles. Some were painted with elaborate patterns of colors, but most were the shade of a camel crossing a desert.

People were bustling up and down the sandy street. But these weren't just any people. Their skin was a rich caramel color, as if they'd been kissed by the sun. The men were shirtless, and they were wearing white linen skirts or sarongs that fell just above the knee. Some were bald, others had thick black hair, but they were all clean-shaven. One man was herding goats with a long stick, others carried chickens in cages on their backs and pushed carts full of produce and grain.

The women wore long, plain shifts of white, but their necks and wrists were adorned with copper, silver, and gold jewelry that jangled when they moved. Many were carrying large clay pots on their heads or gathering up naked children who had stopped to scoop up sand and sift it between their fingers.

A man selling fish out of a large basket glared at Daniel and

Abigail with a suspicion one might give to outsiders. Luckily for them, the man soon found himself sidetracked by a rather loud woman with silver bracelets up to her elbow trying to barter for his fish with a pair of woven sandals. They were speaking a strange language. And in the strange world of time travel, Daniel understood every word.

"Um...Daniel," Abigail said, balancing herself with her arms as if the earth beneath her was unstable.

"Right," he said, looking around.

He had a pretty good idea where they were, but he wanted to be certain. He motioned for Abigail to follow him, and they curved in and out of the busy streets until they came to the marshy edges of the city where a giant river snaked rapidly through the arid land. The river water had spilled over its banks and had surrounded the palm trees and reeds that grew along its edges.

"Just what I thought," he said.

"Where are we?" she asked, sounding uncertain.

He squinted against the blaring sun, shading his eyes. "Well..."

Abigail's face flushed like a ripe peach. "Well, what?"

"If I were to guess by the large river that's clearly in flood stage—I'd say...ancient Egypt?"

Abigail's expression darkened.

*Uh-oh.*

He hurriedly flipped to the back of the book to the return portals and scanned down the list with his finger, looking for Egypt. His finger stopped where only an *Egy* was visible under a watery brown stain. He dared not tell Abigail the return portal was unreadable.

He grimaced. "I think we're barking at a knot here."

Abigail threw up her hands. "What does that mean?"

He closed the book and stuck it back in his pants pocket. "It means..."

"Yes?" she hissed.

"No return portal for Egypt."

In one swift movement she was in his face, clenching his shirt with her hands. He had to admit, the strength by which she had taken hold of him was impressive.

"Would this be the right time to remind you that this was your idea?" he asked meekly.

She gritted her teeth and pushed him away. "Argh. I'm so stupid. I knew we should have made a plan. We should have studied the portals, rechecked return portals, made lists—"

"I prefer the word foolish to stupid," he said, interrupting her.

She pointed a finger at him. "Stop talking."

He clamped his mouth shut.

She stared at the river. "We should have known by the painting. Moses was pulled from the Nile, and now we're likely standing right next to what appears to be the NILE!"

He chuckled nervously. "That's right, Moses turned its water to blood, didn't he?"

She ignored his attempt at humor. "Clearly the Italian painting portal is not your way home," she said. "And if there's nothing in your little red book on how to get back, how are we supposed to—"

Daniel held up a hand, trying to calm her. "Don't worry," he said. "There are plenty of Egyptian structures that still exist in present day. One of them has to be a portal."

She stared at him for a moment, brows furrowed. "Yes, you're right," she said, snapping her fingers. "The pyramids for one."

"Great idea," he said. "Now we just need to figure out *where* in Egypt we are."

"How big can Egypt be?" she asked looking around.

"Bigger than North Carolina," he said gingerly.

Abigail's face reddened and she abruptly spun around and walked back toward the city. Well, more like stomped if he were going for accuracy.

"Where are you going?" he asked, chasing after her. His shoes quickly filled with sand. He stopped briefly to remove his shoes and socks. There was nothing he hated more than sand in his shoes.

*This* small tidbit he knew about himself. His last name though? No.

"Wait!" he called after her. Her leaving him behind was becoming a pattern. He ran after her and quickly realized the mistake of removing his socks and shoes.

The sand was *hot*!

He hotfooted it past Abigail and fell in the sand at her feet, stopping her in her tracks. He tossed his shoes aside and quickly put his socks back on. Almost immediately, a small monkey with a large fig in his mouth scuttled past them, grabbed one of Daniel's shoes, dropped the fig in it, and carried the shoe away like it was a serving dish.

The scowl on Abigail's face slowly disappeared and was replaced by a small smile as his humiliation unfolded. She held out a hand and helped Daniel to his feet.

"Well, that's not something you see every day," he said, brushing himself off.

"I'm sorry I got angry," she said.

Daniel nodded. "It's okay."

"No, it's not. When I get scared..." She gave him a tentative look, as if she were debating whether or not to complete the sentence. "Never mind. It won't happen again."

But he didn't need her assurances. He was scared too. With each portal that he tried, the prospects of returning home grew dimmer.

# CHAPTER
# EIGHTEEN

*Thebes, Egypt*
*609 BC*
*Merypath – with Djedmut*

Mery held her mother's hand as they walked along the avenue of sphinxes that led to the Karnak Temple. Six large, multicolored statues of Ramesses II loomed ahead. Two were seated by the entrance, and the other four Ramesses statues stood along the tall walls that surrounded the holy grounds.

Mery had walked this path many times. Djedmut was faithful to Amun, creator and protector of life, and she brought Mery to his temple several times a week to pray. They seldom saw her father, Jahi, when they came to the temple, even though he was a priest there. Often his duties were private and not meant for the eyes or ears of the common man. The god Amun had a big appetite though; she knew that. Her father had often talked of how long the daily meal offerings of bread, meat, and fruit took to prepare. Once the ka (spirit) of Amun partook of the offering, it was also her father's duty to distribute the food to the other temple priests or to the tombs of important officials so that the ka of the departed would have food to sustain them in the afterlife.

A large number of people were heading to and from the temple, but in the midst of all of this, she sensed someone *or something* with strange ka. She casually glanced over her shoulder and caught sight of a pale-skinned boy and girl, both wearing strange clothes. Neither was barefoot. One had clothing on his feet, and the other had on some kind of closed sandal. It was true there were many foreigners who lived in Thebes, but these two looked out of the ordinary.

The yellow-haired girl elbowed the boy in the side and they both stared at Mery with a look that she associated with getting caught doing something one shouldn't be doing. She was tempted to investigate further, but she couldn't let herself get distracted as she was often prone to do. She had to find out where the Pharaoh wanted her mother to go and why. She loved her father, but Jahi had been pushing for a favorable marriage for Mery ever since she'd turned fourteen, and Djedmut wasn't going to be able to hold him off much longer. What if he arranged a marriage while her mother was gone? Mery couldn't let that happen. She wanted to be a scribe like her mother, not a wife of some nobleman or priest. Her writing lessons would stop if she married. Surely, Seshat, the goddess of wisdom and writing, would make sure that didn't happen. She prayed another prayer of protection and squeezed her mother's hand.

# CHAPTER

# NINETEEN

"Did you see that girl staring at us?" Abigail asked.

"I'd stare at us too. We kind of stick out," Daniel said, looking down at his stockinged feet. He focused in on the temple ahead of them. It would be the clue they needed as to what part of Egypt they were in.

"Why can't we just ask someone where this is?" Abigail said.

"Oh, that wouldn't draw attention to us at all. You should do it," he suggested. "Run up there and ask that girl and her mother. You think they know English?"

"Sarcasm doesn't suit you," she said.

It suited him just fine. In fact, he rather liked it. *Hates sand. Likes sarcasm.* The clues to his identify were endless.

"Shouldn't these human-headed lions be a big clue?" Abigail asked. "I mean, how many roads are lined with hundreds of sphinxes where you can also see the Nile river?"

"Um, pretty much all of Egypt runs along the Nile. But the sphinxes do suggest that this is probably ancient Thebes."

"How do you know this stuff?" she asked.

"I spend a lot of time reading about the history of the art pieces. The art museum has a small library, you know."

"It does?"

He sighed. "I have to know as much as possible or I could get stuck in the past."

"Or the future," she added.

"Touché."

"I know that word," she proudly announced. "It means you admit I made a clever point."

"You like words, huh? I learned that one from one of the museum's library books."

She shrugged. "I kind of collect them."

*Words make her happy. Duly noted.*

As they got closer, the size of the temple gates morphed into what he could only describe as gargantuan. He was almost positive that this was the Karnak temple complex, which meant they were in Thebes. The multiple statues of Ramesses II along the temple walls and the two 80-foot-tall obelisks covered in hieroglyphs standing just before the temple entrance were a huge clue. The walls surrounding the temple were covered in colorful artwork that depicted a pharaoh in his chariot, fighting foreigners.

"This is more amazing than Disney World," Abigail said.

"What's Disney World?"

"Never mind. I keep forgetting you're from another time."

They passed between the two obelisks and then the two seated giant Ramesses statues and entered the temple. Once they were inside, they found themselves in a giant courtyard surrounded by multicolored columns.

Daniel's arms tingled with goosebumps. *Parts of the Karnack temple still exist. This could be our way home!*

He reached out and touched Abigail's arm. "This is definitely Thebes, and this is the Karnak Temple. We may be able to get home from here."

Abigail smiled. "What are you waiting for! Say the portal password."

The courtyard was full of people—singing with uplifted hands, clutching their amulets in prayer, kneeling in thoughtful contemplation.

"Not here," he said. "I'm worried we'd accidentally take someone with us. A squirrel accidently came back with me from Spain. If you can imagine the trouble a loose squirrel in the art museum caused, imagine what bringing back an ancient Egyptian would do."

"Good point," she said.

He caught a glimpse of the girl who had turned and stared at them earlier. She and a woman he had only guessed was her mother, based on their similar appearance and age difference, were headed straight toward what he believed was called the Great Hypostyle Hall. If he remembered correctly, regular citizens weren't allowed any farther than the main courtyard, so the hall would likely be empty.

"Come on," he said, tugging at Abigail's arm.

They stayed just far enough behind so that the mother and daughter didn't notice them.

A man with a shaved head standing by the hall entrance nodded to the woman with recognition, and the girl and her mother were allowed to pass into the hallowed hall. When Daniel and Abigail tried to pass by, the man held up a hand and shook his head. Just as Daniel thought, ordinary citizens weren't allowed. They smiled politely and retreated back behind a courtyard column and waited. Eventually the guard strayed into the courtyard and took up a conversation with a temple priest. Daniel and Abigail took advantage of the brief distraction to slip inside.

Shafts of light poured into the hall's center aisle from dozens of small windows high above. Gigantic columns ran down each side of the aisle, and only slightly less gigantic ones to their left and right lined up for what seemed like miles—a hundred and thirty-four columns as a matter of fact. They were thicker and taller than any tree he'd ever seen. The only word he could think of to describe them was colossal.

"This is unbelievable," Abigail said.

They both craned their necks to look at the dizzying heights of the column capitals that had been fashioned to look like papyrus plants blooming at the top, stretching for the sun. Every column was completely covered in fine, colorful etchings and paintings of pharaohs, gods, and bands of hieroglyphs—a wonderful display of greens, blues, reds, and yellows.

"It feels like we're ants," Abigail said quietly.

They ventured left, farther into the darker portions of the hall until they were sure they were alone among the giant pillars of history.

"Okay. Let's see if this is our way home," he said.

Abigail grabbed his hand.

"This place is beautiful," she said as if saying good-bye.

Daniel wasted no time saying the portal password that had gotten them there. "*May we find the favor of him who dwelt in the burning bush.*"

He waited for the feeling of falling, for the darkness and loss of senses.

Nothing happened.

"Try again," Abigail said, squeezing his hand a bit too tightly.

He repeated the password a little louder.

"Who dwells in the burning bush?" a small voice asked.

Abigail dropped Daniel's hand. They gaped at the girl standing in front of them. It was the girl who had been walking in front of them outside—the one who had glared at them over her shoulder.

The girl smiled, seeming quite satisfied with herself at having caught them off guard and in a place that they clearly shouldn't be. Her skin was smooth and unblemished, and her hair was long and black—beautiful against her white shift. She had black eyeliner under her lower eyelids, small, gold hoop earrings in her ears, and gold cuffs on her upper arms. She was wearing sandals now. Before, outside, she'd been barefoot.

"I'm MeryPath," she said, "but I prefer Mery."

Daniel bit his lip. How was it that the girl could understand them? There was no way she knew English. She had to be hearing them in Egyptian. This was *new* in his time travel world. In Calais, the people had heard him and Abigail in English, not French, which was why they had suspected them of being spies. Still, it would better if they didn't talk to her.

"I'm Abigail."

Daniel gave Abigail a look of disgust. She shrugged.

"And you are?" Mery asked, taking a step toward Daniel.

"Daniel," he murmured.

"Where are you from?" Mery asked.

*The 1800s, give or take a hundred years.*

"We're visiting from Greece," Daniel said quickly before Abigail could say something she shouldn't.

"Hmmm," Mery murmured, eyeing his socks.

An awkward silence ensued.

"Do you know how we can get to the pyramids?" Abigail asked.

Daniel sighed. Abigail knew nothing about the art of subtlety.

Mery cocked her head. "You wish to see the tombs of our great pharaohs?"

"Yes, exactly," Abigail said.

"It's a long journey to the north."

Daniel took Abigail's hand and tugged her gently back toward the exit to the courtyard. "Well, we've got to run. Lots to do and see," he said hastily.

*The last thing we need is a curious Egyptian.*

"Why did you have to be so rude?" Abigail asked as she stumbled after him.

"Because we aren't on vacation, and unless you want to get stuck here, we really should move on." Before they could take one more step, Daniel froze.

Standing twenty feet in front of them between the pillars was a woman with dark eyes and a raven ponytail—the same woman who had been in Calais's square when Daniel and Abigail were listening to the governor's speech about surrendering to King Edward. They had only narrowly escaped her grasp then. He'd seen the same woman in Spain when he'd gone through the *Man Scraping Chocolate* portal by himself. She'd shown up looking angry right before he'd spoken the portal password to return back to the museum. He supposed he should have mentioned this to Abigail sooner.

Abigail spotted her at the same time. "Daniel. Is that the same woman who grabbed us in Calais?"

"Yes, that would be her."

Abigail gave him a curious look. "I knew it. You've seen her before Calais, haven't you?"

"Maybe."

"Now what?" she snapped.

Daniel's heart raced. They *could* outrun her. They'd done it before in Calais.

The woman in black moved toward them, balling her small

hands into fists. Her menacing frown and angry stride added to the panic rising in Daniel's chest. As much as he would have liked to know who she was and what she wanted, he wasn't about to put Abigail in danger. And this lady had danger written all over her face.

"Wake—" Abigail said.

"Snakes!" Daniel yelled.

They took off running, weaving around columns, changing directions, hoping to lose the woman. When they thought they had lost her, they stopped briefly and pressed their backs against a column.

"What does she want?" Abigail whispered breathlessly.

"I don't know."

Just ahead, light poured in from the courtyard, casting a large beam across the tiled floor. If they could get outside of the temple, the woman wouldn't have a chance against their young legs.

"We'll run straight through the courtyard and out of the temple. You ready?" he asked.

Abigail nodded. "Ready."

They sprinted toward the light. Daniel pushed himself, his legs burning. Abigail stayed right on his heels. They were going to make it. The warmth of the light spread across his face. They'd go to the pyramids, say the portal password, and all would be well. A warm, satisfied feeling came over him. The plan was solid. They were going to escape the woman in black, *again*. Until...

*Wham!*

Something hit him square across the chest and he fell backward, his head slamming into the floor. He blinked. A blurry image of the woman in black rubbing her left arm stood above him.

Abigail was tugging at Daniel's sleeve, trying to help him up.

"It's time to stop running." The woman's voice was robotic and lacked emotion.

Daniel grasped Abigail's arm and she helped him up. His feet were unsteady. There would be no running this time. They were trapped.

The woman held out her hand. "The red book."

# CHAPTER
# TWENTY

Daniel and Abigail shared a look of dismay. They needed that book if he was ever going to get home. They both knew it.

"What red book?" Daniel said. Playing dumb was worth a try.

"You took something that belongs to me. I want it back."

*The red book? That's what this is all about?*

Daniel took a tentative step back. "I don't have it."

The woman glared at Abigail. "We, um, hid it. We knew you wanted it."

*Not bad.* Daniel had to give her credit for quick thinking. If they could stall her and lure her out of the temple on the premise of going to get the red book, they'd have a better chance of escaping. The woman gritted her teeth and grabbed Daniel.

"Let him go!" Abigail cried out.

The woman searched Daniel, checking his pants pockets, patting down the waist and legs of his pants. To Daniel's complete shock, he didn't have the red book.

Abigail's mouth fell open.

*Please tell me you have it,* he thought, looking at her pleadingly. She shook her head. An unpleasant knot formed in his throat.

*I must have dropped it.*

The woman pushed Daniel away and took Abigail by the wrist, jerking her close. Abigail's eyes widened with fear. "If you don't want your friend to get hurt," the woman said to Daniel, "you'll come along without a fight this time."

"We'll take you to the book," he said, knowing it was a lie.

The woman tightened her grip on Abigail and motioned with her head toward the courtyard. Abigail gave Daniel a desperate look. His mind raced.

*How are we going to get out of this one?*

Just as the three of them stepped out into the courtyard, Mery and her mother blocked their path.

"There you are," Mery's mother said, smiling at Abigail as if they were old friends. "We've been looking everywhere for you two. I know it's easy to get lost in such a grand place. You really shouldn't be in the hall. It's only for priests."

The woman in black shifted uncomfortably. But before she could do or say anything, Mery's mother held out her hand to Abigail. The woman in black reluctantly released her, and Abigail stepped forward.

"Thank you for helping them find their way out. I apologize. I should have told them the hall was forbidden."

Then Mery's mother turned and walked across the granite floor of the courtyard with a gentle hand pressed against Abigail's back. Daniel followed, letting out a huge sigh of relief even as his mind raced with worries about losing the book and the implications of interacting with the Egyptian girl and her mother.

Mery took up close beside him, rubbing shoulders with him. She pushed something into his side. He glanced down.

"You dropped this," she said softly.

His spirits immediately lifted. He took the red book and slid it stealthily into his pants pocket, for fear the woman behind them would see it.

"Thank you," he said.

They locked eyes. In the light of day, she was even more beautiful. She had her mother's eyes—dark as midnight. Mery smiled at him, and he quickly looked away. He wasn't going to get charmed the way Abigail had with Prince Edward in Calais. He was above that kind of thing.

Wasn't he?

Mery and her mother said nothing as their party of four walked down the avenue of sphinxes back into the narrow, crowded streets of Thebes. Shortly after, Daniel lost sight of the trailing woman in black.

They eventually entered a section of flat-roofed, two and three-story homes surrounded by outer walls that were nearly six feet tall. Some walls were painted with hieroglyphs and others were solid shades of pale yellow and blue. Egyptians could be seen on the roofs of their homes, eating under canopies made from palm leaves.

Daniel peeked inside some of the residences that had left their gates open. Their inner courtyards teemed with life. But there was no grass here in the desert. The Egyptian yards were stone, sand, or tile. Pots were planted with palm, flowers, or vegetables. Some yards had a small section fenced off for chickens and goats.

The smells of the Egyptian neighborhood were equally exotic—a mix of animal, clove, and onion. The sun heated the sand, lending its own hint of dusty earth. The ancient city of

Thebes was unlike anything he could have ever imagined. The Egyptians were a beautiful and vibrant people, and they had turned the desert they lived in into an oasis. Daniel became lost in a kind of symphony the city was playing before him. His heart calmed as the threat of the woman in black faded.

After a long walk that left Daniel feeling tired and thirsty, Mery's mother stopped at a wooden gate surrounded by white walls full of hieroglyphs. She rapped lightly on the gate and a young man opened it to reveal a majestic, tiled courtyard teeming with life. Daniel and Abigail followed Mery and her mother as they strode straight through a handful of chickens searching for bugs. The flightless birds flapped their wings and scattered. Two goats chewed straw in a corner shaded by a large in-ground palm. A female sitting cross-legged by the home's open doorway was kneading bread dough up to her elbows in a wooden bowl while a boy picked figs from a tree planted in a decorative pot.

They passed through the large opening into the living quarters. The ceiling was supported by a single wooden column in the middle of the room. The floor was covered with a rug and assorted colorful pillows for seating. A table held some clay vessels and cups, along with a vase of palm leaves. But the most notable feature of the room was the small niche in the back wall that held two carved statues. One had the head of a hippo, a big stomach, the legs and arms of a lion, and a tail like a crocodile. The other statue looked like a bearded, bowlegged dwarf sticking out his tongue.

"Tawaret," Mery said, "the one with the hippopotamus head. She is a goddess who protects women during pregnancy and childbirth. And the other one, Bes, is a protector of children and home. Mother said they helped me come into the world, and now they watch over our home."

"Very interesting," Daniel said, meaning it.

A young barefoot boy in a white pleated sarong came into the room and bowed. His head was completely shaved except for a single black ponytail that hung to one side.

"Gyasi, get our guests something to eat. Some bread and fruit will do. Oh, and honey if we have it."

"Yes, Lady Djedmut."

Daniel choked immediately upon hearing the woman's name. He coughed uncontrollably, unable to clear his throat. Abigail slapped him on the back. Djedmut quickly went to the table and poured some water from a clay vessel into a cup and handed it to him. He drank greedily, though his coughing had nothing to do with being thirsty.

*Djedmut.*

He not only knew the name; he knew her eternity box—her coffin. Daniel had practically memorized the hieroglyphs on the coffin at the museum in his attempt to learn how to read the strange markings.

*To the ka of the Osiris lady of the house Djedmut, true of voice...*

*Can this really be the Djedmut on the coffin in the museum?*

He doubted it. Still...was it possible?

"Feeling better?" Djedmut asked.

Daniel nodded, but he couldn't help but stare at her now. She was healthy, young even. She didn't look like someone about to die. There were probably thousands of women named Djedmut in ancient Egypt. He ran the dates of the coffin through his head.

The young servant brought in a large iridescent blue platter, smooth as glass. It had a round loaf of bread on it along with figs and a small bowl of what he presumed was honey. The boy placed the food on the floor in the center of the array of pillows and left the room.

"Please," Djedmut said, motioning for Daniel and Abigail to sit.

Daniel knelt and sat cross-legged on a pillow. Mery planted herself next to him. Djedmut sat next to Abigail across from them.

Now that he was seated, he was able to relax a bit. Mery and Djedmut had saved them from the woman. *Mrs. Black*, Daniel decided, since her hair and clothes were as dark as the night sky.

"Thank you," he said, "for helping us."

Djedmut folded her hands together. Her gold bracelets jangled lightly. "Mery said you were lost and needed help."

Daniel looked over at Abigail.

How much should they say? What should they say? It was important not to say or do anything that would change history.

Abigail gave him an *I got this* look, then she turned to Djedmut.

"We were traveling with our parents," she said. "We stopped in Thebes for supplies and Daniel and I got lost. Then that woman at the temple tried to kidnap us."

Daniel sighed inwardly. The story was a little dramatic for his taste. His brown hair had some blonde highlights so he supposed they could pass for siblings. And technically they *were* lost.

"That is horrible!" Mery said.

"Yes, it is." Djedmut said.

Daniel thought he detected just a hint of doubt in her voice.

"We will say a prayer to Horus thanking him for keeping you safe," Mery said.

"If you could help us find another boat going north," Daniel said. "I'm afraid ours has certainly left by now. Our parents said if we ever got separated, we should meet at the pyramids."

"We can help them, can't we, Mother?" Mery asked. "The temple has boats."

Djedmut stood, a slight frown on her face.

"We would be so grateful," Abigail said. "And so would our parents."

Daniel bit playfully at his lip.

*Please let this work.*

"It just so happens I'm traveling north this afternoon," Djedmut said.

Mery bolted up. "What does Pharaoh Necho want with you?"

"MeryPath!"

"I'm sorry, Mother. I saw his name on the scroll that was delivered this morning."

Daniel sensed that he and Abigail were intruding on what should have been a private conversation between mother and daughter.

Djedmut's face reddened, but after a few awkward seconds, she calmed. "The Pharaoh needs an interpreter. I must travel north immediately."

"But he has scribes and interpreters! Why you?"

"He has a specific need, and his interpreter is ill."

Fear spread across Mery's face. "Necho is leaving to take an army to help the Assyrians. Everyone in the city is talking about it. He's going to help the same monsters that came and destroyed Thebes!"

Djedmut remained silent but her expression suggested that she found Mery's behavior unsettling.

Mery shook her head over and over. "Surely Father will refuse to let you go. It's too dangerous." Tears pooled in her eyes.

"You don't turn down a request from the Pharaoh. Necho is descended from the very gods themselves!" Djedmut snapped.

Mery let out a sob and fled from the room.

Djedmut managed a weak smile. She gestured to the food. "Eat. We have a long journey ahead of us."

# CHAPTER
# TWENTY-ONE

T he royal banana-shaped boat sent by the Pharaoh, Necho II, to take Djedmut north to Zau bobbed at the edges of the Nile like a colorful rainbow. Its sides were a checkered pattern of red, blue, and white, while the curled tips of the bow and stern shimmered in gold. A small gold and white cabin stood in the middle with a large mast emerging from its center. The vessel's rich appointments were like a shout compared to the whisper of the humble reed fishing boats floating down the river.

"Wow," Abigail said as they walked up a ramp and boarded the Pharaoh's boat.

Daniel grunted while lugging one of the many baskets that Djedmut had brought with her. The thing weighed as much as a good-sized boulder. Thankfully, her servants followed with the rest of her things.

Djedmut remained on shore and talked to the boat's crew about Daniel and Abigail. Daniel waved awkwardly and smiled. The men didn't look happy, but after a few more

words, it appeared the matter of him and Abigail riding along
had been settled, and Djedmut headed toward the boat.

"Looks like we're in," Daniel said.

Abigail ignored him, and instead roamed the floating
palace, touching all the rich surfaces and poking her head into
the cabin at the center.

He followed her. "Try not to say too much else on the way
to the pyramids," he reminded her.

"I know. Don't change history," she said.

Djedmut's coffin crossed his mind again.

"I feel bad for Mery," Abigail added. "She was really nice."

"If it weren't for her," Daniel said, "who knows what *Mrs.
Black* would have done to us."

Abigail stopped her inspection of the boat and faced
Daniel. "Speaking of the strange lady, who is she and what
does she want?"

Daniel shrugged. "She showed up the first time I went
through a portal and now appears to be following me."

"But you've never seen her at the museum?"

"No. Never."

Daniel patted his pants pocket just to make sure the red
book was safe and secure. "She said the red book belonged to
her. When am I going to remember the past?"

Abigail put a sympathetic hand on his shoulder. "You will. I
just know it."

"What if I'm a horrible person? I mean, what if I stole the
book?"

"You're not a horrible person. You must have had a good
reason for taking it."

"I wonder."

She squeezed his shoulder then let go. "We'll keep trying to
find your home. Don't worry, okay?"

He nodded, but with each new portal he was feeling less hopeful. How was he supposed to not worry?

Djedmut boarded the boat and approached them.

*To the ka of the Osiris lady of the house Djedmut, true of voice...*

"Pharaoh's men have agreed to drop you off at Giza."

"Thank you," Daniel said, "for helping us."

She smiled a beautiful white smile that made her dark eyes shine. "No doubt, Shai, our god of destiny, has put you in my path. Our lives are bound together now."

*In more ways than one. Thousands of years from now, hundreds of thousands will look upon your coffin and know your name.*

Daniel knew that this was the Djedmut from the art museum as soon as Mery had said the Pharaoh's name. *Necho.* The time period fit the coffin—25th dynasty. Abigail seemed to sense that he was struggling with something and gave him a strange look.

*Should I tell Abigail about Djedmut?*

No. The less she knew, the less likely she'd be tempted to change history.


That night they slept on the stern of the boat on reed mats. The stars sparkled above them while the boat moved silently through the water. Men held torches at the bow to guide the way. Djedmut sheltered inside the cabin but had pulled back the white curtains of its windows to let in the night air. The spicy smelling oil from her small lamp wafted across the boat. She was seated cross-legged with a wooden ledger on her lap. Over and over, she dipped her thin reed into the ink she had mixed on a small palette and made short, delicate strokes on a piece of papyrus paper.

Daniel eventually dozed off, soothed by the current of the

Nile. He dreamed that the woman in black took the red book from him and burned it in a blinding fire.

He woke suddenly when someone jabbed him in the ribs. He shot up, ready to give Abigail a piece of his mind, but he was greeted instead by large eyes that weren't hers. A hand clasped over his mouth before he could cry out. As soon as his eyes adjusted to the moonlit deck he recognized the face.

*Mery?*

Abigail sat up, rubbing the sleep from her eyes. "Mery?"

"Keep your voices down," Mery whispered, looking nervously toward the now darkened cabin.

"What are you doing here?" Daniel asked.

Mery sat down and crossed her legs. "I don't know. I wasn't thinking. I just climbed into one of my mother's baskets."

Daniel recalled the heaviness of the basket he'd hauled onto the boat and how his arms now thoroughly ached. For some reason, he found himself feeling annoyed by her sudden presence.

Abigail was clearly not feeling the same way. She reached out and took Mery's hand. "Don't worry. Your mom will understand."

"You don't know Djedmut. She will be furious that I disobeyed her."

"Maybe you should have thought of that before you stowed away," Daniel said grumpily.

Abigail furrowed her brow at him. He rubbed his aching arms.

"She's going to war," Mery explained. "I was afraid I'd never see her again."

Daniel swallowed the lump in his throat. Was he really bothered by Mery's presence, or did he just fear that her worries about Djedmut would prove to be true? What if the war was where Djedmut would lose her life?

"We're here for you," Abigail said.

Daniel sighed then laid back down and rolled over while the two girls chattered into what remained of the night. Having Mery there was only going to make it harder to keep his secret. Every time he'd look at her, he would be thinking of Djedmut's coffin sitting at the museum. This was very different than Calais. There, he knew that the men who had volunteered their lives to save the city would live.

Djedmut wouldn't be so lucky.

# CHAPTER
# TWENTY-TWO

The warm breezes that had traveled miles across the Egyptian desert did little to diminish the sweltering heat on their trip down the Nile. Daniel had ditched his clothes for an Egyptian kilt and sandals, offered to him by one of the Egyptian soldiers, a week into the journey. Even though it was weird to walk around shirtless, he was too hot to care. He'd thought that he would tan, but instead he stayed a bright shade of pink.

Djedmut had modified a long, sleeveless dress for Abigail and tied back her unruly hair. She'd even given her a simple silver bracelet to wear and painted black kohl under her bottom eyelashes. At least for now, he and Abigail fit in as well as they could.

Mery had suffered through her mother's lecture on obedience and spent a good part of the first week sulking. Her mother was putting her back on a boat to Thebes as soon as they arrived at the pyramids.

The second week into their journey, the boat floated into the ancient port of Giza—home of one of the eight wonders of the world. Daniel could scarcely form a sentence as the Great Pyramids came into view. The three towering pyramids were sparkling white with golden tips at their peak. They shimmered in the sunlight, as if made from millions of crushed diamonds. It was beyond anything he could have imagined. How was it possible for the ancients to build such giant structures?

"Wow," Abigail said. "This is incredible!"

For a moment, the three of them all seemed to have forgotten their troubles. Mery was smiling and no longer sulking after being thoroughly scolded by Djedmut for secretly slipping aboard. Abigail had stopped worrying about being gone from the museum too long. Daniel had finally convinced her that it wouldn't matter how long it took them to get back to the museum—no time would have passed. And he'd even stopped thinking of Djedmut's death.

Mostly.

They'd spent the last several days becoming friends with Mery. Djedmut had even taught them how to mix inks and let them try writing on pieces of broken pottery with her long reed pens.

"Our ancestors built great tombs for themselves," Djedmut said.

Daniel hadn't noticed that Djedmut had silently slid up beside him.

"It's marvelous," he said, knowing that one day this would be nothing more than ruins.

"I must depart soon after we arrive."

"We'll be fine," Daniel said.

"Yes," Abigail said, chiming in. "Thank you again for helping us."

Djedmut looked at Mery. "I will see the priest at the temple where we'll be docking. He'll make sure you get back home."

Mery's good mood vanished.

Djedmut left them and went to talk to one of Pharaoh's soldiers.

Abigail took Mery's hand. "We'll always be friends."

Mery looked at Daniel. "Yes, maybe Osiris will allow all of us to work together one day on one of his great buildings."

Osiris was the god of the underworld—the place after death for the ancient Egyptians.

"Your heart will weigh true," Daniel said, thinking it was the best compliment he could give her. For the Egyptians believed that when they died, their heart would be weighed against a feather. If their heart was lighter than the feather, it proved them worthy enough to enter the afterlife.

Mery smiled, but her eyes welled with tears. "And may Osiris find you true of voice."

His throat swelled with emotion. He knew the saying. It was on Djedmut's coffin. To be *true of voice* meant you were honorable. He didn't feel honorable.

Abigail pulled Mery into a hug, and Daniel walked down to the end of the boat to compose himself. Was it honorable not to warn Djedmut of the potential danger that might lie ahead for her?

*Don't throw a pebble into history...* His own words to Abigail haunted him.

Their boat was guided alongside a floating dock by Pharaoh's men using long poles. A temple stood high above them and the Nile. Men on the dock knelt and reached out guiding hands, drawing the boat even closer. A narrow plank of wood was lowered into the boat. Daniel, Abigail, Mery, and Djedmut disembarked and climbed a stone staircase up to the white temple.

At the top of the steps was a beautiful balcony tiled with elaborate mosaics of palm trees and lotus flowers. Large pots covered in hieroglyphs were filled with flowering plants and trees. Ten feet below the stone railings of the balcony, the Nile swirled, and Ibises skimmed its waters looking for their midmorning meal.

"I'll go inside and speak to the priest," Djedmut said to Mery. "He'll arrange for you to return to Thebes."

Mery hung her head and nodded.

Djedmut smiled at Daniel and Abigail. "I wish you safe journeys. May Horus protect you and your family."

Daniel shifted awkwardly, but Abigail rushed forward and hugged Djedmut tightly.

"Thank you for everything," she said.

Once Abigail backed away, Djedmut glanced at Mery, but instead of offering her mother a heartfelt goodbye, Mery's face reddened. She turned and ran into the temple. Djedmut followed silently. Daniel wanted to call after Mery and tell her that this might be the last time she'd see her mother alive, but he couldn't. History had already had its say.

"We should go make sure Mery is okay," Abigail said, adjusting her cross-body bag.

Daniel nodded.

They found Mery in a long, columned room. The walls were painted with life-sized renderings of the Pharaoh and gods of the afterlife. Daniel recognized the jackal-headed god, Anubis, and the hawk-headed god, Horus. Smoke drifted up toward the ceiling from an altar dish, releasing a spicy sweet scent into the air. Mery was leaning up against one of the pillars like it was nothing more than an abandoned park bench.

"You should go find your mother and father," Mery said as they approached.

"We can wait with you, until the priest comes," Abigail said.

Daniel nudged Abigail in the side. He was anxious to move

on. They needed to get to the pyramids and back to the museum.

"No. I'll be fine," Mery said, clinging to the amulet around her neck.

Abigail looked pleadingly at Daniel. When he didn't say anything, Abigail narrowed her eyes and tightened her lips.

He shrugged and mouthed "What?"

"Can you excuse us a minute, Mery?" Abigail asked, not waiting for a response before dragging Daniel by his elbow out of earshot.

"Can't you see how upset Mery is?" Abigail asked.

He studied the frown on her face. Annoyed or angry he wasn't sure, but *he* was definitely annoyed. "Yeah, well, there's nothing we can do about it. She shouldn't have snuck aboard in the first place." He said it with as much snark as he could muster.

Abigail clenched her teeth. "How can you be so heartless?" she snapped.

Something burst inside him. "Maybe because Djedmut is going to die, and we can't get caught up in this because this is history," he whispered harshly.

The color drained from Abigail's face. "What?"

Daniel tried to swallow the lump that had formed in his throat.

"Djedmut dies?" she asked.

Guilt spread from Daniel's gut all the way to the tips of his ears. "Abigail..."

Her hand shot out, and she placed a finger on his lips. "How could you keep this from me?" she whispered urgently.

He mumbled. She reluctantly removed her finger. "I thought it would be easier if you didn't know."

She stared at him for a few seconds, her anger fading. "It

must have been hard knowing all this time and acting like everything was fine."

"It was hard," he said, scratching absently at his sunburnt chest.

"How does it happen?" she asked sorrowfully.

"I don't know. Djedmut's coffin is in the museum. The timeframe fits, but it's hard to say if it's soon or years from now."

"But you think because she's going with the Pharaoh to war that this could be where she...dies?"

He nodded.

"Poor Mery. She didn't even say good-bye to her mother. What if she never sees her again?" Abigail asked.

Daniel sighed. That was the wrong thing to do. Abigail's brief moment of sympathy vanished, and she stormed off in a huff.

He returned to find the girls hugging, and Abigail assuring Mery that they would stay with her until her boat left for Thebes. Mery looked expectantly to Daniel, but when he offered her no reassurance that he was on board with the plan to wait, a scowl darkened her face.

*Great. Now both of them are angry at me.*

"I'm going out front to get some fresh air." He almost laughed when he said it because he knew he'd be inhaling a lungful of sand as soon as he stepped out of the temple. They glared at him.

*Why did I blurt out that Djedmut was going to die?*

But wasn't a part of him glad not to be the only one carrying the burden of knowing? Telling Abigail had been self-ish. Now she would suffer with the knowledge too.

He found the front of the temple and stepped outside into a wave of heat. A fine dust blew across his face and he spit into the wind. He reached down and scooped up a handful of hot sand.

*Welcome to Egypt*, he thought, but quickly realized someone had actually spoken it. He looked over. The woman in black, *Mrs. Black*, was standing only a few feet away. Her dark eyes were calm, but her body was stiff and angry.

Daniel's pulse quickened. *How is she always able to find me?*

"Don't think of running," she said.

"What do you want?"

"You know what I want," she grumbled.

Daniel reflexively reached for his pocket with his sand-free hand, but his Egyptian kilt had no pockets. For a brief second, he'd forgotten. Abigail had the red book. She was keeping it in her satchel along with their old clothes. He didn't know what to do, so he improvised.

"I lost it," he said.

"Why don't we ask your friends? Maybe they know where it is." She smirked.

Daniel hated smirks. Without thinking, he threw the sand in his hand into Mrs. Black's face and ran back into the temple. He could hear her cursing and spitting behind him.

*Bull's-eye.*

"Abigail! Mery!" He screamed as loud as he could, racing back toward the galley. The girls met him in the hallway.

"What is it? What's wrong?" Abigail asked frantically.

"The..." He couldn't breathe. He couldn't talk. Mery gently took his arm, trying to steady him.

"The...?" Abigail said.

But he didn't have to say anything more. Abigail's eyes widened as the woman came into the hallway still wiping at her eyes.

"Mery," Abigail said calmly, "get us out of here. Now!"

All traces of sulking disappeared, and Mery sprang into action. "This way!" she said, grabbing Abigail's hand. They took off running back toward the exit to the courtyard on the Nile.

"Yeah, sure. Don't worry about me!" he yelled. He raced after them, wondering what they were going to do when they got outside. There was nowhere to go except into the Nile. And frankly, he knew what was in that water, because it had been their toilet and bath water the whole way to Giza.

Daniel caught up with the girls outside at the stone railing. The three of them stared down at the rapids of the Nile. It was still flood season and the water had a strong current. Djedmut and the Pharaoh's boat were gone.

"Now what, geniuses?" Daniel asked.

The woman in black stepped out into the courtyard and headed straight for them, hard and fast, teeth gritted, ponytail swinging.

"Only one way out," Mery said as she climbed on top of the railing.

"Uh..." Daniel stammered.

*Do I know how to swim?*

Abigail climbed up to join Mery.

Daniel stood still and stared straight into the eyes of Mrs. Black.

"Daniel, come on!" Abigail shouted, holding out her hand to him.

He turned and took Abigail's hand and climbed up. It was a lot farther down than it looked.

"Wake—" Abigail said.

"Snakes!" Daniel shouted.

They all jumped at once. The next thing Daniel knew, he was holding his breath and kicking and paddling to the surface of the water.

*I can swim!*

If he hadn't been under water, he would have sighed with relief.

The three of them surfaced around the same time, and they were instantly swept away with the current to the north. The woman in black gazed down at them, then hit the stone wall with her hand in frustration.

*Bye-bye, Mrs. Black. Who's smirking now?*

Daniel's merriment in having escaped the woman was quickly tempered by reality.

*The pyramids!*

They were floating away from their way back to the museum.

# CHAPTER
# TWENTY-THREE

Daniel, Abigail, and Mery were rescued by men on a large trade ship, similar to a barge, that was carrying sacks of grain and beans, acacia wood, and jars of nut oil. Daniel panicked when the crew refused to take them back to the pyramids and suggested they be dropped off at the nearest city, but Mery convinced them that the Pharaoh himself would reward them for taking them all the way north to Zau, the current capital and home of the Pharaoh—Necho II. In Zau, Mery could find her mother and Daniel and Abigail could find a ride back to the pyramids.

Exhausted after their long dip in the Nile, the three of them collapsed onto the deck and sat back against a stack of wood—Mery sandwiched in the middle. They panted and swiped the water from their faces like a trio of wet cats.

By some miracle, Abigail had managed to hold onto her bag, which meant the red book was still in their possession. Before they had boarded the boat to Thebes, he'd watched her root through her bag and pull out a clear crinkly thing she called a baggie. She'd put the book inside it and assured him it would protect the book from any water mishaps. Hopefully that had held true.

They were quiet for a while, perhaps because they were each contemplating their predicament. Mery was no doubt thinking that she was drifting farther away from home instead of toward it. Abigail was surely thinking the same thing he was —that their way back to the museum was behind them at the pyramids. Things just felt...hopeless.

"Who was that woman back there at the pyramids?" Mery finally asked. "And why is she after you?"

Abigail leaned forward and looked at Daniel. She lifted an eyebrow as if she were curious how he would explain Mrs. Black without mentioning time travel. He didn't know if it was the exhaustion, the heat, or what, but an unexplained anger swelled inside him.

So, he spilled.

"We're from the future," he growled. "And that woman back there has been chasing us through time because apparently she's after my red book, which I supposedly took from her, but I can't remember because I've lost my memory, and we thought the pyramids were a portal back to the future, but clearly we never had the chance to find out, and now we're here and we're wet, hot, and tuckered out on a boat that may or may not take us to Zau, and we'll probably be stuck in Egypt forever, and frankly my complexion is just not made for this much sun, so I'll probably die from heat stroke!"

He took a deep breath.

"And...I HATE SAND!"

Abigail's mouth fell open and her face flushed a bright red. Well, that was his initial assessment, but the longer he looked at her, the more she looked like a wildebeest ready to charge.

Mery narrowed her eyes at him. "Really?" she asked. "You're from the future?"

"Yes, really," he said with a little too much attitude.

Mery turned her head to Abigail for confirmation.

"Don't throw a pebble into history, huh?" Abigail said, frowning at Daniel.

He shrugged, feeling somewhat satisfied at baring his soul.

"Yes, it's true," Abigail said to Mery. "But Daniel is acting more like he's from Mars than from the future."

Daniel clinched his fists at Abigail's dig.

"Mars? Where is that?" Mery asked, looking back and forth between.

Daniel remained silent and so did Abigail. The tension between them was almost visible.

"I believe what you say is possible," Mery finally said.

"Why?" Abigail said, sounding exasperated. "I'm not even sure I believe it."

"It's your clothes, the way you look," Mery said. "Your Egyptian is bad. Some of the words you say I've never heard before. The gods are very powerful, perhaps they sent you to help me."

Daniel sprang to his feet. "Highly unlikely!"

Abigail pushed herself up. "Stop, Daniel."

They glared at each other, water still dripping down their faces. Mery rose up between them with her bright smile and calming hand. Daniel knew he was being ridiculous, but he couldn't help himself.

"Why can't you just be kind and help someone for a change," Abigail said. "All you ever think about is yourself."

He winced at the sting of her words. Didn't he have good reason to only think of himself? He didn't even know who he was! But then he looked into Mery's eyes. They were kind and dark and beautiful. *She* was beautiful. And if he were honest, maybe he had been harsh with her because he didn't want to care about anyone that he'd have to say good-bye to.

Daniel wiped a hand down his face, clearing the remnants of the Nile. "I'm sorry, Mery," he said. "Abigail is right. I've been unkind to you."

Mery lowered her eyes. Abigail's expression softened at his words. Suddenly they were all standing there, lost. It was then that Daniel knew what they needed to do.

"Before we leave Zau, we're going to help you find Djedmut. You should be with your mother." He didn't know if Djedmut would die soon, but he was going to make sure that Mery had what time was left with her mother.

"Are you sure?" Mery asked.

Abigail beamed.

"Yes. I'm sure," he said.

Mery rushed into his arms and hugged him tightly. Her hair smelled of mud and earth. But he didn't care. He knew then that he was going to do anything he could for Mery, even if that meant he'd never find his way back home. Abigail came in and hugged Mery from behind, and they stood there, the three of them together making one big sandwich, ready to conquer the world.

"Anybody else hungry?" Daniel asked sincerely.

# CHAPTER
# TWENTY-FOUR

"I don't understand why Zau is considered lower Egypt," Daniel said. "It's *north* and Thebes is to the south. Thebes should be lower Egypt."

Mery smiled, and he tried to avoid looking into her onyx-colored eyes.

"It's because the Nile runs south to north," she said sounding amused. "If the river flowed from the north to the south, then what you said would make sense."

"You're both making my head hurt," Abigail said.

Daniel had only really argued with Mery for argument's sake. He'd just wanted to hear her talk of Egypt. Besides what else was there to do on a boat? For the past two days, Mery had talked of Zau and how the city's favored goddess was the war goddess, Neith. They tried not to talk of war, but it was clear that Mery had strong feelings about the Assyrians that Pharaoh Necho was leaving Egypt to help. Fifty some years ago, they had ravaged Mery's city, Thebes, killing and taking the riches of the city. Since then, Egypt had been basically a vassal of the Assyrians, which was just a fancy way of the

Assyrians saying, "We'll let your Pharaoh continue to rule Egypt, but you'll help us when we tell you to or we'll come back and conquer you again." Now Necho was sending his army to help the hated Assyrians fight the Babylonians. Peacemaking was a strange business in ancient Egypt.

"What's the plan when we get to Zau?" Abigail asked.

Daniel stuck out his chest and lifted his chin. "We march up to the palace and demand to see the Pharaoh!"

Abigail rolled her eyes, but Mery laughed. He grinned with contentment at having made her happy. The truth was, he had no idea what they should do once they got there. He wanted Mery to be with Djedmut, but he certainly didn't want to get caught up in a war, not after Calais.

Soon after arriving in Zau, it quickly became clear that they were in another predicament. The Pharaoh and his thousands of infantries and chariots had already left Zau and were headed to aid the Assyrians at Carchemish, which was northeast and miles from the relative safety of Egypt. That meant Djedmut was also gone.

Abigail wrung her hands and eyed Daniel nervously. Mery held on to her amulet and murmured prayers.

"What now?" Abigail asked quietly.

He didn't know if it was fate, or divine intervention, but the men that they had been traveling with were loading the ship's contents onto wooden carts pulled by donkeys. When Daniel had inquired where they were taking the supplies, he got the answer he was looking for.

"The ship's cargo is going to Necho's troops," Daniel told the girls.

Mery's face lit up.

"I don't know," Abigail said, sounding unsure.

"We'll catch up to Djedmut," he explained. "Reunite mother and daughter, and then we'll come back to Zau and find a boat to take us back to the pyramids." He grinned trying to appear confident.

"Oh, please!" Mery said, turning to Abigail.

Abigail nodded, though the little lines that had formed between her eyes showed her uncertainty.

"Surely the war goddess Neith will protect us," Mery added.

Daniel and Abigail shared a look but said nothing. Neither was about to tell Mery that her gods would all fall away into history one day.

After much wrangling, Mery managed to secure their passage with the supplies by offering up Daniel's red book. She showed the soldiers the book and explained that the Pharaoh's scribe, Djedmut, had forgotten it and must have it. What could the soldiers say? The book was unlike anything they'd ever seen, and it was filled with words they couldn't recognize. They took it for safekeeping, which put Daniel ill at ease. He told himself that they were doing the right thing for Mery, but the farther away they got from the pyramids, the more he doubted he would ever find his way home.

# CHAPTER
# TWENTY-FIVE

I f Daniel had been forced to describe the next few weeks to anyone, he was sure he'd have no words that could sufficiently express the madness that came with traveling miles and miles across desert-like terrain with the sun beating down on your neck. It didn't help that his skin refused to tan. He burned and peeled. Period. There was no fading to a golden hue as Abigail had done. He was perpetually pink. The soldiers had taken to calling him Mau (meow), the Egyptian word for cat, because he was always grooming himself by constantly peeling off his dead skin. He had tried his very best not to do it, because if they caught him, a chorus of meows would break out followed by raucous laughter. Who knew the ancient Egyptians had a sense of humor?

He was thankful when their journey finally ended at a place called Megiddo where the Pharaoh and his army were currently camped. But the hope for a happy family reunion between mother and daughter quickly faded. Djedmut was neither happy nor angry to see Mery.

It was worse.

She was lying unconscious in a tent. She'd been bitten by a poisonous snake three days ago.

Daniel and Abigail stood a few feet away while Mery knelt at Djedmut's side, weeping and praying to her gods. Djedmut had been stripped of her fine jewelry and makeup. A green amulet with a snake head and a human body hung singularly around her neck. It was Nehebkau, a snake-headed god thought to also have power over snake bites.

Abigail burst into tears and ran out of the tent. Daniel followed her outside. She wrapped her arms around herself and hung her head.

"We did our best to get Mery here in time," he said unconvincingly.

Abigail swatted at her tears. "We should have told her."

"Told her what? That Djedmut dies? All of these people are technically dead."

"You know what I mean," she spat. "We could have prepared her somehow."

"She might live," he added, though even as he said it, he knew his words were half-hearted. Abigail nodded, but they both knew the odds were against it. Proper medical treatment for snake bites had not yet been discovered in ancient Egypt.

Three bare-chested, sandal-shod soldiers with spears approached them. Their furrowed brows told Daniel that whatever it was they wanted, it was serious.

"Are you the children who brought the red book?"

Word traveled fast in Pharaoh's camp.

"Mau?" One of them asked, looking at Daniel.

He bristled at the unfortunate nickname. "Daniel," he corrected.

"Come with us. The Pharaoh wishes to see you."

Both he and Abigail hesitated. Could they really leave Mery

at a time like this? When neither of them moved, the soldiers prodded them with the blunt ends of their spears.

"I guess we're going," Daniel mumbled, and they reluctantly followed Necho's men.

The Pharaoh was tucked away inside a surprisingly ordinary tent. The temporary shelter was much larger and grander than the small tents in the camp, but there was nothing especially royal about it. There were a few small tables inside. One held platters of bread, fruit, and dried fish, and the other was home to small statues of their gods with shallow bowls of burning incense.

Necho was seated on a wooden chair draped with an off-white sheepskin. He appeared to be bald, as no hair showed beneath his blue leather headdress. His dark eyes were lined in black kohl, and his gaze followed their movements like a keen-eyed hawk. Several amulets hung down his bare chest, all made from precious green and blue stones. Daniel and Abigail were given a gentle push forward. Abigail glanced nervously over at him.

*What does the Pharaoh want with two kids?*

When they were within a few feet of Necho, the soldiers pressed down on Daniel and Abigail's shoulders with their spears, forcing them to their knees. They knelt and bowed their heads, though Daniel had no idea what the proper protocol was for greeting a pharaoh.

"Rise!" Necho said.

They rose slowly, uncertain of what was to come. That's when Daniel saw it.

The red book.

*His* red book in the Pharaoh of Egypt's hand!

And this was where everything went wrong.

"Yeah, about that," Daniel stammered. "It's not worth a hill of beans."

"Silence!" Necho cried, rising to his feet.

Abigail punched Daniel in the arm which got a mixed reaction from the Pharaoh. Something like shock and annoyance.

Necho opened the book randomly and held it out to Daniel. "Read it."

He had no choice but to take the book. As soon as he saw the page that Necho had handed him, his face flushed.

*What are the odds that Necho would turn to this specific page?*

Abigail snatched it out of his hands. Necho raised an eyebrow.

"Girls can read too, you know." She read with an air of defiance. "*May we find the favor of him who dwelt in the burning bush.*"

Daniel's vision disappeared with a flash of light. He quickly grabbed Abigail's arm. His mind melted into darkness. His stomach flipped and churned as he traveled through the vast chasm of time. Here he was weightless, and thought was dreamlike. And then, just like that, he was on firm ground again.

He blinked a few times, only mildly aware of Abigail standing next to him. It took a moment for them both to gather their composure. They were standing right in front of Djedmut's coffin at the art museum. He sighed with relief.

"What just happened?" Abigail said.

"There must have been something, some small artifact in that tent that exists in the modern-day world."

They both examined their clothes. They were just as they were before they had left. Abigail was back in her "Meh" T-shirt and jeans with her cross-body bag. Daniel was back in his jacket and hat, and the red book was securely in his pants pocket.

Everything was as it should be.

He dared a small smile. "We're back Abigail." He could scarcely believe it.

"We're back," she said returning the smile.

"Where is the great and powerful Osiris?" A loud voice boomed behind them.

A chill crept over Daniel. "It couldn't be," he whispered.

He and Abigail shared a look of pure fear. They turned around slowly.

There, right in the middle of the art museum's Egyptian galley, stood the Pharaoh of Egypt, Necho II.

# CHAPTER
# TWENTY-SIX

"Okay, don't panic," Daniel said, though his heart was racing so hard that he thought his rib cage might explode.

"We just brought the Pharaoh of Egypt back with us!" Abigail hissed.

A frowning, gallery security guard was heading straight for the Pharaoh.

"Thoth! Come weigh my heart!" Necho cried out to the ceiling.

To Daniel's surprise, he was still hearing Necho in English. Which meant so was everyone else.

"What do we do?" Abigail pleaded. "Necho thinks he's passed on."

Daniel chewed on the inside of his cheek. "We take him back to Egypt."

They both fast-walked toward Necho, trying to stay cool and not run like a couple of kids. All they needed to do was get him back to the *Finding of Moses* painting in the Italian galley, say the portal password, and they'd be back in Egypt.

He hoped.

They each took Necho by the arm, something completely inappropriate for someone of his rank, but necessary.

"What is this?" Necho said, trying to shake them off. "Why are you here?" he asked, his brow furrowing with confusion. "Who are you?"

"We're here to take you back," Daniel said. "There's been a mistake."

"Mistake?" Necho asked. "What does this word mean?"

*Great.*

The guard was closing in. There wasn't much time.

Necho let himself be led by them, but Daniel could see that he was taking in the floors, the tall ceilings, and the Egyptian artifacts. The muscles in Necho's arm tightened beneath Daniel's grip with each step.

*He's starting to figure out that this isn't his underworld.*

They were about to exit the gallery when a tour group showed up and blocked their path.

"Mom, look at the man!" one of the kids said.

"This is so cool," someone said. "A live-action exhibit."

Necho ripped himself from Abigail's and Daniel's grips. They were losing control.

"You must kneel in the presence of a pharaoh!" Necho shouted to the group.

There were a few chuckles. Cell phones (the strange devices Daniel had learned about early on but had yet to fully understand) rose up in a wave, followed by clicking noises.

"Kneel!"

A few in the crowd looked at each other, but after a moment of hushed whispers, they all knelt.

*They think this is an act. They're playing along.*

This gave Daniel an idea.

Abigail whispered to Daniel out of the side of her mouth. "What is happening?"

The guard in the room stopped his pursuit a few feet from them, confusion on his face.

*If the guard thinks this is part of the tour, this may be our way out.*

Daniel sprang into action. He took a step forward to address the Pharaoh's audience. "Rise and meet the great Pharaoh Necho!"

Abigail's mouth fell open, her eyes wide.

"Come on," Daniel chided the stunned group, "don't be shy."

One by one the people rose to their feet.

Daniel spoke softly but firmly to the Pharaoh. "We came here by mistake, but if you do what we say, we can get you back. You have a war to attend to." They had to get him back or all of history would be changed. Sweat pooled on Daniel's forehead. Necho frowned, but he gave a grunt of assent.

"This," Daniel bellowed, trying to sound theatrical, "is the great Pharaoh Necho II of Egypt!"

Necho stood a little straighter, stuck out his bare chest, and raised his chin.

*Perfect.*

"He is some pumpkins!"

Abigail looked at him with wide eyes and shook her head. A few folks exchanged confused looks.

*Right. No 1800s slang.*

He cleared his throat. "He is a mighty warrior and leads great armies!"

Just like a well-rehearsed play, Necho crossed his arms. Cell phones clicked away.

"He built the first canal in history, connecting the Nile River to the Red Sea."

Necho looked over at Daniel and gave him a confused look. Technically, the work on the canal had stopped because he had to go help the Assyrians, but it would get finished by the Persians.

"Now, we must go so that the Pharaoh can get back to his important work. A messenger has just arrived with news from his Assyrian allies."

The group broke out into applause and parted like the Red Sea as Daniel and Abigail led Necho out of the Egyptian exhibit. Once they were well into the center gallery, Daniel sighed with relief.

"I can't believe it," Abigail said quietly. "That actually worked!"

"Where are we?" Necho asked.

"Somewhere you shouldn't be," Daniel said. "But you'll be home soon."

"Who's in the burning bush?" Necho said, referencing the words Abigail had only spoken minutes ago in the Pharaoh's tent.

Daniel hesitated. He couldn't just say God. The Egyptians had so many.

"Yaweh," he said, using a Hebrew word for God.

Necho stopped in his tracks. This drew unwanted stares from people walking the long hall.

"You know the Hebrew god?" Necho asked.

Daniel wasn't sure if this was some kind of trick question. "Yes?"

"Good. You can interpret for me."

*That's what he needed Djedmut for? To interpret Hebrew?*

Then it hit him. The history—the reason why the Pharaoh needed a Hebrew interpreter. This was where Daniel should have said he didn't know Hebrew. But they were stopped awkwardly, drawing too much attention, and all he wanted to do was to get Necho back to Egypt.

"Sure. Whatever you need, but we need to go. Now." That seemed to satisfy the Pharaoh, and they pulled him a little more forcefully than they really should have back to the European gallery to find baby Moses.

Daniel's palms sweated with nervous anticipation. He glanced over at Abigail on the other side of Necho. Her face was white with fear. The Pharaoh *had* to go back; they both were feeling the horror of the situation.

They hurried into the European gallery and stepped up to Luca Giordano's painting. There, for Necho's viewing pleasure, was a very white princess of Egypt standing in her regal gown gazing down at the pink baby Moses.

Necho's eyes widened. "What is this?" He tried to draw closer. This drew the attention of another museum guard who had just entered the gallery.

Daniel tried to pull Necho back, but he shook him off.

"This looks like the Nile River, but these people, their clothes..."

Abigail glanced nervously at the guard who was now very focused on the three of them.

"Say the portal password," Abigail demanded. "The guard is coming."

"Who are these fair people?" Necho continued, speaking to no one in particular.

"What about the guard?" Daniel asked. "He'll see us disappear."

"We don't have a choice!" Abigail said raising her voice.

Necho reached out a hand and touched the baby Moses.

The guard ran toward them.

They had no choice; they couldn't afford to get detained. There would be no explaining an ancient Egyptian Pharaoh.

Daniel and Abigail each grabbed one of Necho's arms. He fought them, but they held on with everything they had. The guard was only a few feet away. It was now or never.

*"May we find the favor of him who dwelt in the burning bush."*

With a flash, Daniel fell into oblivion. He spun, traveling back through thousands of years. Distant thoughts ran through his head. What if they landed back in Thebes? What if they went someplace else, some other time? What if they couldn't get Necho back into his historical time line?

Just as quickly as the thoughts came, Daniel's feet became solid beneath him. The swirling slowed and his eyesight cleared. To his relief, the first thing he saw was the Pharaoh's makeshift throne in the tent they'd left minutes earlier. The second thing was the shock on the Pharaoh's advisors' and attendants' faces. They all immediately fell to their knees and dropped their heads to the ground in reverent awe.

Necho stood between him and Abigail, wobbling a bit.

"Your Majesty," one of his advisors said, rising. "You disappeared before our very eyes, only to reappear instantly."

Necho nodded. "Yes, yes. Something strange has happened here." He stared at Daniel and Abigail in awe.

Abigail turned to Daniel. "That was..."

"A close one?" he said, finishing her sentence.

She nodded and they smiled at each other, but their smiles quickly faded as they examined each other. They were wearing their American clothes. The trip back had reset everything. Abigail had her bag across her shoulder and the red book was safely tucked away in Daniel's pants pocket. Necho and all his staff stared at them with wide eyes and whispered urgently to each other.

How were they going to talk their way out of this one? One minute they were dressed like Egyptians, and the next they looked like creatures from another planet. Abigail's tan was even gone, and Daniel's skin was no longer sunburned. They were as fresh as the first time they'd arrived. But that wasn't the worst of it.

"We have a problem in the European gallery," a loud voice boomed.

Daniel's muscles tensed, and Abigail let out a short gasp. They slowly turned around. A dark-skinned man with commanding biceps towered over them. His black pants and royal blue polo shirt told them all they needed to know. They'd brought a museum security guard with them over two thousand years into the past!

CHAPTER

# TWENTY-SEVEN

The museum guard pressed his finger to his ear. "Security, do you read me?"

"You're not at the museum," Daniel said matter-of-factly.

The guard, who looked to be in his late thirties, took a look around, absently rubbing his stomach. He took a deep breath and blew it out slowly. "I knew I shouldn't have eaten those jalapeño poppers last night."

Pharaoh Necho and his advisors observed this ongoing display in a kind of shocked silence.

"Excuse me?" Daniel said.

"Jalapeño poppers. Every time I eat them, I have nightmares." He clenched his blazing white teeth as though he had gas.

"You think you're dreaming?" Abigail asked.

"How else would you explain this?" he said with a sweep of his hand.

Daniel and Abigail grinned at each other. At least they wouldn't have to try to explain the unexplainable.

"Silence!" Necho shouted.

Daniel winced. He had momentarily forgotten that they had taken the Pharaoh to the future and back. But the bigger question, and the one that trumped any concerns over what the Pharaoh was thinking, was how they had gotten back to the museum in the first place? He surveyed the tent. Outside of the small tables and some reed baskets, the only other large piece was the makeshift throne. Sparse as the contents of the tent were, there had to be some artifact in the tent that existed in the current world.

A sour-faced Pharaoh exchanged hushed words with his advisors.

"Are you thinking what I'm thinking," Daniel whispered to Abigail.

"That this time travel stuff is totally messed up? Yeah."

"No. That our way home is in this tent. We just have to figure out what artifact it is that took us back."

"Time travel?" The museum guard asked with curious interest.

"How do we figure that out?" she asked, ignoring the guard. "It literally could be anything. A tooth. A ring."

Daniel scratched his neck. "Why was Necho the only one who went back with us?"

"Hey!" the museum security guard said next to Abigail's ear. She jumped causing Daniel to jump. "Are you saying we time traveled to ancient Egypt from the art museum?" He scanned the room with a suspicious eye.

"Yes," Abigail said. "That's what we're saying."

Daniel sighed. The last thing they needed was a meddling art museum guard.

"Maybe he can help," Abigail said, shrugging one shoulder.

"I'm Capability Brown," he said, sticking out his hand between them.

"Capable?" Abigail asked, shaking his hand.

He flashed a wide grin. "Capability. But you can call me Cap. Makes it easier to remember than five syllables."

Abigail smiled. Of course, *she* liked five syllable names. Any word with any syllables for that matter.

Cap shoved his warm hand into Daniel's. But Daniel wasn't feeling quite as enthusiastic about their new friend. How were they going to manage the Pharaoh, Cap, and getting back to the museum?

Necho finished consulting with his advisors and resumed his kingdom-ruling by sitting on his throne and glaring at Daniel, Abigail, and Cap.

"Uh-oh. Mr. Egyptian man doesn't look happy," Cap said.

"He's a pharaoh," Daniel said, gritting his teeth. Abigail was biting her lip, suppressing a smile. Daniel was not amused. The museum guard was going to be trouble.

"Let me handle this," Cap said, stepping forward. "Sir, we can explain. You see there's been an anomaly in earth's magnetic field, likely causing a temporary portal..."

"Silence!" Necho stood, his neck turning bright red. "I will deal with you two—you *three*, later. Right now, I've got an Israelite army standing in my way and I must address their king. Whatever magic you just did will be discussed another time."

Daniel sighed with relief. Explaining what had just happened and why they were in their futuristic clothes with the addition of a very loud man was not a conversation he nor Abigail were ready for. Ever.

"Bring in the Hebrew messenger," Necho instructed the soldier standing by the entrance. The soldier was a bald, bare-chested man with a large sword strapped to his waist. Daniel thought he recognized the god of war, Neith, among the many amulets the man wore around his neck.

Abigail grabbed Daniel's arm and pulled him over to the side. "What's going on? What Israelite king?"

Daniel's history was slowly coming back to him.

"This is Mediggo. And if I'm right, there's a large Israelite army waiting to attack. One led by King Josiah."

Abigail widened her eyes and dug her nails into his arm. "We can't be here for this," she said in an urgent whisper.

"We don't have a choice," he reminded her.

"But...but this is...biblical!"

She said the last word a little too loudly, and Necho shot her a warning look.

Daniel tried to talk without moving his mouth. "That's why we need to figure out what the artifact is that got us back to the museum so we can get out of here."

She released his now throbbing arm and nodded. "You're right," she said softly, lowering her eyes. "What about Mery and Djedmut?"

They both had grown close to Mery. Leaving without saying good-bye would be hard. *Really* hard. The one thing that he'd wanted to avoid had become unavoidable. He'd developed certain feelings for Mery.

"I don't know." And he didn't know. Not knowing anything about his past or his future seemed to be the only thing he did know.

Pharaoh's soldier ducked back inside the tent and bowed slightly. "Your Majesty, the messenger refuses to come to your tent."

"For what reason?" Necho demanded. The soldier shifted uncomfortably.

"This is getting interesting," Cap said, sliding over to Abigail and Daniel. He had somehow pilfered a piece of fruit from the small table and gingerly popped it into his mouth.

The soldier glanced over at Cap with a slight scowl, but

quickly returned his attention to the Pharaoh. "The messenger does not want to defile himself by being in the presence of pagan gods."

"Defile," Abigail whispered. "To make unclean or impure."

"I know what it means," Daniel said between gritted teeth.

Cap offered Abigail a high five which she happily accepted. How had Daniel lost control so fast?

"We will go outside to meet this messenger," Necho said, seemingly not bothered by the demand.

Abigail reached for Daniel's hand as they waited for Necho to exit first. Daniel squeezed her hand, trying to reassure her that all would be well.

*If only we could figure out what had gotten us back to the museum.*

As Necho passed by them, Cap pointed to the amulets hanging around the Pharaoh's neck. "That green one there is the snake god, Nehebkau. There's one just like it at the museum."

It was similar to the one Djedmut had been wearing— snake head and human body.

Then it hit Daniel.

Abigail must have seen the look of joy on his face. "What? Did you figure out what got us back to the museum?"

Daniel grinned. "Necho's amulet of Nehebkau."

Abigail turned her attention to the Pharaoh as he exited.

"Cap's right," Daniel said. "There's an amulet just like it at the museum. So, if I had to guess, I'd say the museum amulet is the exact one Necho's wearing."

"It can't be," she said. "What are the mind-blowing odds that it's the same amulet at the museum?"

They were prodded to follow behind the Pharaoh.

"Then why was he the only one to go back with us?" Daniel asked. "The tent was full of other people."

She nodded. "You have a point. Only one little problem."

"What's that?"

"How do we get the amulet away from the Pharaoh?"

Daniel's stomach twisted and turned. She was right. They'd never get close enough to Necho to snag the amulet.

Cap placed a hand on Daniel's shoulder and leaned in between them. "You need that necklace to get us back to the museum?" Cap asked quietly.

Daniel cringed. For a moment he'd forgotten Cap was there.

"Today's your lucky day," Cap said.

"What do you mean?" Daniel asked, not sure he wanted to know the answer.

"If that's the way back, I can get it for you," Cap said, keeping one eye on the Pharaoh.

Daniel and Abigail shared a look. "How?" they both said at the same time.

Cap grinned widely and rubbed his hands together. "You just leave it in the capable hands of Capability Brown."

Abigail smiled. Daniel frowned.

*We're never going to get back to the museum.*

# CHAPTER
# TWENTY-EIGHT

"You can't steal the amulet from the Pharaoh," Daniel said to Cap. Why did it feel like he was scolding a child?

"Who said anything about stealing?" Cap said with a scowl. "I'm a man of incorruptible good character."

Abigail's eyes beamed at his use of a big word. "Incorruptible...?"

"It means I can't be swayed to do that which is wrong." He looked fixedly at Daniel as if he was making some kind of a point.

"We don't need your help," Daniel said.

"By the looks of your predicament, I'd say you do."

Abigail tugged at Daniel's sleeve and whispered in his ear. "Maybe it wouldn't hurt to hear what he has in mind."

*Great. Two against one.*

The discussion about plans to abscond with the amulet would have to wait. They had arrived at the edge of the camp where the Hebrew messenger waited. Daniel didn't know what he was expecting, but the messenger had come alone.

He was youthful in appearance with curly dark hair and a full beard. He was wearing what looked like a short-sleeved white dress that fell above the knee, but there was tight-fitting leather armor over the top of it. Tied around his waist was a blue sash and a leather belt with a scabbard that held a short sword. The laces of his leather sandals were tied around the braces on his shins.

He was battle ready.

Two Egyptian soldiers demanded his sword. The messenger removed his belt and freely gave it over. He then knelt before the Pharaoh on one knee and offered up a beige scroll.

Necho plucked it out of his hand and the man stood.

"You two," Necho said, addressing Daniel and Abigail.

*Oh no. Did I say I could interpret Hebrew back at the museum?*

Abigail gave him an uncertain look, but they had no choice. They stepped forward.

Necho broke the seal and handed Daniel the scroll.

"Read."

Sweat broke out on Daniel's forehead and his hand shook as he accepted the scroll. Abigail looked over his shoulder as he unrolled the parchment. The strange symbols were unreadable.

"Your Majesty. We can't read Hebrew," Daniel confessed.

Necho scowled at them. They had just transported the Pharaoh forward in time using what he thought was great magic, but they couldn't read a simple message. Daniel feared what would come next. To their surprise and relief, Mery came running into their midst. "Djedmut's awake!"

Abigail rushed into her arms. Daniel sighed with relief.

*You won't be leaving this world today, Djedmut.*

He placed a reassuring hand on Mery's back. She released Abigail and pulled him into a tight hug. She smelled of flower blossoms despite the sweltering heat. He closed his eyes. He wanted to remember her like this—happy.

Mery pulled away and the three of them stood there smiling at each other, united once again in friendship.

"The physician says she'll live," Mery said excitedly.

"We shall take the scroll to Djedmut!" Necho pronounced.

Daniel had forgotten they were in the middle of a critical situation, and Mery, finally realizing what she had walked into, flushed a light pink.

"Is she strong enough to read it?" Abigail asked Mery, as if that would stop the Pharaoh from proceeding.

Mery nodded. "I think so."

Relief made its rounds, and the whole contingent of advisors, soldiers, attendants, and Josiah's messenger followed Necho, weaving through the camp of tents and Egyptian soldiers.

"Aren't you going to introduce me to your friend?" came a booming voice next to Daniel's ear. He grimaced.

*Cap. How do I explain this one?*

Mery glanced back. "Who is that?"

*Yes, Daniel. Please explain that you traveled to the future and brought back a meddling security guard, who could at any second set history spinning by saying or doing virtually anything.*

Mery eyed Daniel's and Abigail's clothes, then Abigail's cross-body bag.

"Something's happened," Mery said.

Abigail nodded.

Cap stuck a hand between them. "Name is Capability."

Mery looked at his hand with uncertainty.

"They don't shake hands here, Cap," Daniel said grumpily.

"And you are young lady?" Cap asked.

"MeryPath."

"We'll explain later," Abigail whispered to Mery.

"Is he from...you know...the future?"

*What gave it away?*

"It's hot as blazes out here. You have any sunscreen in that bag of yours, Abigail?" Cap asked.

"Sunscreen?" Mery said.

Daniel frowned. "Ignore him if you can."

Thankfully they arrived at Djedmut's tent and that stopped the Cap show. Necho, Mery, Daniel, and Abigail were the only ones allowed inside the small tent. They hovered over Djedmut, while Mery dropped to her knees and held her mother's hand.

Djedmut opened her eyes and smiled at her daughter, then her eyes drifted upward and widened upon seeing the Pharaoh.

"We have Nehebkau to thank for your recovery," Necho said.

She nodded wearily.

"I have a Hebrew scroll that needs to be interpreted if you are able."

"Of course," she said weakly, raising a hand to receive the scroll.

Mery pushed her arm down. "I can read the scroll," Mery insisted.

"Mery—"

"Let me try, Mother. You can correct me if I'm wrong."

Necho scowled but nodded his assent and handed Mery the scroll.

She unfurled it and held it so her mother could also see it as she read.

"Pharaoh Necho," Mery began, "you will not be allowed to pass through Judean territory. Take your army and return to Egypt or face us on the hills of Mediggo upon which no foreign sword will pass. This in my hand, King Josiah of Judea."

Djedmut raised a hand and placed it on Mery's cheek. "Well done, Mery." Then she closed her eyes and fell asleep.

Necho spun around and left the tent with the three of them on his heels. He informed his advisors of the message, and they talked in hushed tones. The Israelite messenger waited patiently.

Necho approached Mery. "Can you write a message to King Josiah?"

Mery wrung her hands. "I don't know. Djedmut has taught me Hebrew, but I can speak it better than I can write it. It would be better if I delivered the message in person."

Necho's advisors whispered harshly in his ear.

Daniel and Abigail pulled Mery to the side. "Are you sure about this, Mery?" Abigail asked. It was a dangerous task, and Daniel was pretty sure this was *not* how it was supposed to play out in history.

Mery nodded, though little lines of worry tugged at the corner of her eyes. "This is my destiny—to be a scribe like my mother. If I do this for the Pharaoh, who knows what could happen."

Daniel bit at his lip. Mery in an Israelite camp with two armies on the brink of war?

"It's too dangerous," he said.

Much to his dismay, Necho motioned for Mery to return to his side. "Show me," he said pointing at the messenger. "Tell him his god, Yahweh, came to me in a dream and told me not to delay our journey. Will he oppose his own god?"

Mery looked over at the messenger, and hesitated, but only for a moment. She strode up to him and said something in a language that Daniel didn't understand. The messenger, taken aback by this small girl's use of Hebrew, looked around as if uncertain of what was expected of him. He replied and bowed slightly at the waist.

"What did he say?" Necho asked. This sent his advisors into a fury of objections of which Daniel caught a word or two, most referring to Mery as a child and a girl. Necho dismissed the complaints with a hand. Mery remained calm in the midst of the tirades.

*She knows who she is and what she wants.* That was more than he could say for himself. It made him admire her all the more.

"He said he will take me to deliver the message of your dream to King Josiah if that is your wish," Mery said.

Necho seemed to ponder while his advisors delivered their final assault of disapproval.

"Mery," Daniel pleaded, taking her gently by the arm. "There's going to be a battle. A big one."

"Daniel!" Abigail exclaimed.

He wasn't supposed to do or say anything that would change history, but this was Mery they were talking about sending to King Josiah. It was his fault she was there in the first place. How could he let her walk into danger? Yes, Djedmut would live for now, but would Mery? Daniel's face flushed. How did he explain the real reason he didn't want her to go?

*I don't want to lose you. Not like this.*

Mery's eyes were full of determination, drive. There was nothing he could say that would take that from her ka—her spirit.

"I can do this Daniel. Don't worry. The goddess Neith will go with me and deliver me safely back."

He smiled weakly. Abigail put a supportive hand on his shoulder.

The small group grew quiet. "The girl goes to King Josiah!" Necho bellowed.

"Then we're going with you," Daniel said without thinking.

"I don't think so," Cap said, dangling the Pharaoh's amulet between them.

"What? How?" Abigail stuttered.

"Like I said, leave it to Capability Brown to get us home," he said with a wide grin.

"This amulet is your way home?" Mery asked.

Daniel nodded.

Mery took the amulet from Cap and placed it in Daniel's palm. "You have a life to live and so do I. This is where our path together ends."

Could he really leave her like this, not knowing if he'd led her to her death? So he said the only comforting thing he could think of.

"Your mother will be adored in the future."

Mery's eyes widened. "How?"

"Daniel," Abigail said laying a cautionary hand on his shoulder.

He shrugged it off. He knew he shouldn't be telling Mery this, but he didn't care. "She will be revered for all of time," he added. Mery smiled, but her brow was knitted in slight confusion.

"It's time," Necho said approaching.

Abigail embraced Mery quickly and they shared a tearful good-bye. Then Mery turned to Daniel, and for the briefest moment it was just the two of them.

"May your heart weigh true," he said, his voice cracking.

She reached out and squeezed his hand. "And may Osiris find you true of voice." Mery wiped her tears away, stood just a little taller, and addressed the Pharaoh. "I'm ready, Your Majesty."

And just like that, Mery strolled away from them and disappeared among the tents with the Israelite messenger and a contingent of soldiers that would escort them to the edge of camp.

"Time to go kiddos," Cap said. "There's some weird lady in a black jumpsuit giving us the stink eye."

Daniel stared at the empty place where Mery had stood, unable to process anything else.

Abigail took him by the arm and shook him. "It's her. The woman in black!"

"You've seen this woman before?" Cap asked.

Daniel blinked and quickly regained his composure. Sure enough, the woman in black was standing just ten feet away, watching them...waiting.

"We better hurry before we lose this chance to go," Abigail said.

Daniel nodded and tied the Pharaoh's amulet of Nehebkau around his neck.

Taking the lead, Cap motioned them to follow. They snuck away from Necho, weaving between tents until they found a private spot.

Abigail took Daniel's hand and reached out to take Cap's. "We have to hold hands," she said. Cap quickly complied.

"Stop!" The woman in black yelled.

"Hurry!" Abigail cried, jiggling Daniel's hand. "Say the password!"

Daniel watched numbly as Mrs. Black ran toward them. How was it that the woman always found Daniel and Abigail in the past, but had never showed up at the museum?

"Daniel," Abigail said jerking his arm. "She'll go back with us if you don't hurry." Before Daniel could speak, Abigail said, *"May we find the favor of him who dwelt in the burning bush."*

Light. Darkness. Swirling, falling, cascading through hundreds of years. He was speeding away from Mery, yet the warmth of the Egyptian sand and the smell of the sweet oils

Mery used on her hair enveloped him. It felt like he was bringing her with him. In a way, she would always be a part of him.

In a flash, the earth became solid beneath Daniel's feet, and he waited for the world to right itself and his vision to clear. He blinked. The three of them were standing in the European gallery.

Cap glanced at his watch, tapping it a few times with his finger.

"How are we going to explain this to Cap?" Abigail said.

Daniel reached for the amulet around his neck. It was gone. Had they changed history or was it still intact?

"We're not." He took off running toward the Egyptian exhibit.

"Wait! Daniel!"

Mery was dead. The past was over, but he had to be sure.

He arrived, breathless, at Djedmut's coffin. He sighed with relief. The coffin was just as it was. They hadn't changed history.

"Daniel," Abigail said, coming up beside him.

"Yes?"

"Cap is following us, and he doesn't look happy."

Daniel retraced his steps and glanced outside the gallery. Sure enough, Cap was striding toward them like a man with a purpose.

"Come on," Abigail said, grabbing his hand. "We need to get out of here and regroup."

"Regroup? Where?"

"My house."

# PART THREE

ABIGAIL AND DANIEL

...SECURE COMM TRANSMISSION TO THE
FANTASTIC ORDER OF ODD TRAVELERS FROM
TRAVELER #2520

...TARGETS LAST KNOWN LOCATION: ANCIENT
EGYPT, 609 BC

...MISSING RED BOOK: CONFIRMED

...PIGGYBACK RIDER: CONFIRMED

...TARGET STATUS: IN PURSUIT

...15:12:29 INTERSTELLAR TIME

# CHAPTER
# TWENTY-NINE

*Abigail*

Abigail and Daniel sat cross-legged on her pink ruffled comforter and shoved take-out pizza into their mouths.

"This is amazing," he said, sounding like he had a mouth full of marbles.

"Yeah, well, try not to get it on my bed." Not that she cared. She had grown out of her pink phase three years ago.

"What do you call this again?" he asked.

"Pizza."

He wiped his mouth on his white sleeve, leaving a streak of grease. She rolled her eyes and handed him one of the paper-thin napkins that came with the pizza.

"Mmm," he mumbled, followed by a huge swallow of his last bite. "Your mom seems nice."

"She's okay. She doesn't understand me."

Daniel gave her a quizzical look.

"Never mind. She's great."

"Did you have to tell her my parents flew to Europe and left me here to fend for myself?"

"How else would I explain you?" She eyed him up and down, "And your appearance?"

He looked down at his attire.

"I told her you ran out of clean clothes and had to wear stuff you found in the attic."

He wiped a greasy hand down his vest. Abigail hopped off the bed and grabbed the white plastic bag of clothes they'd purchased at a thrift shop before picking up the pizza.

"Here you go," she said tossing the bag onto the bed.

Daniel rummaged through it and pulled out a pair of jeans. "I don't know about these strange pants. They feel hard..."

Abigail put her hands on her hips. "You need to fit in. People stare."

He pulled out the blue and white striped polo shirt. "I guess this one's okay."

Abigail resumed her position on the bed. Daniel's red book sat between them.

"Now what?" Daniel asked. "How do we...regroup?"

"We can't just keep trying portals. It's getting too dangerous," she said.

"So, what do we do?"

"I want you to tell me everything you remember, no matter how small."

Daniel rubbed his face with both hands. "I told you I don't remember anything."

She reached out and placed a reassuring hand on his knee. "Okay, let's try it like this. Try to recall every little weird thing that you can think of. Dreams, thoughts. Anything."

He nodded and looked at the ceiling.

"Fire. I dream of fire sometimes."

Abigail picked up the red book and flipped through. "Maybe there's a painting with fire in it?"

"There is. *The Eruption of Mt. Vesuvius* in the European gallery. But it's not in the red book."

"Hey," Abigail said, stopping at the last page. "What's this?" She turned the book to him and pointed. "George Washington by Thomas Sully? It's circled. Does that ring any bells?"

Daniel squinted at the page. "Bells?"

Abigail sighed. "Ring any bells is an idiom. Does it mean anything to you?"

"Other than George Washington was the first president of the United States, no. But I'm pretty sure this painting is not at the museum."

"I have an idea." She bounced off the bed and opened the top drawer of her desk. She pulled out her pink laptop.

"We need to find out where this painting is."

"And how do we figure that out?" he asked with a sigh.

She held up her laptop with one hand. "We have the best deciphering machine known to humankind."

He straightened up, his eyes alight with curiosity. "Machine?"

"Having a computer is like having a secret code breaker," she said. "And all we have to do is feed it the information."

"Kum-pu-ter," Daniel said.

"Com-*pu*-ter."

She sat down on the edge of the bed and flipped it open. He scooted next to her, and they sat side by side.

"I'll key in 'George Washington, Thomas Sully, NC' and see what we get."

"Wow," Daniel said. "So, it's like a book you can ask questions."

"Exactly."

"Add the word *fire*," Daniel said.

"Good idea." Abigail typed lightning fast, and a whole list of search results popped up.

*North Carolina State House - Wikipedia* was the first search engine result. She quickly clicked on it, and they read silently until she spotted a reference to the painting of George Washington.

"Look," she said. "It says the George Washington painting *was hung in the NC State Capitol in 1818.*" Her heart raced with excitement. "Maybe it's still...there," she said, scrolling down.

Daniel pointed at something far more interesting. "On June 21, 1831, while working to fireproof the building, workers accidentally set the roof on fire," he read.

"Fire," they said in unison.

Abigail picked up reading The Raleigh Register account of the fire. "*Awful conflagration! It is our painful and melancholy duty again to announce to the public another appalling instance of loss by fire, which will be deeply felt and lamented by every individual in our State. It is nothing less than the total destruction of the Capitol of the State, located in this city.*"

Daniel fell back helplessly on the bed. "If the George Washington painting was my way home, I'm stuck here forever."

She reached over and patted Daniel's leg. "Sit up. Look!"

"At the very bottom—last sentence. Read it."

"*The Sully painting of Washington,*" Daniel read, "*was rescued from the fire and reinstalled in the new building.*"

He abruptly stood up and began pacing in front of her, rubbing his mouth.

"The time fits—1831," she said. "Your clothes, the way you talk."

He stopped and stared at her.

"Well?" she asked.

He sat beside her again and studied the screen, then

pointed to a painting at the bottom of the screen. "I can't remember anything about a George Washington painting, but this painting here, I'm sure I've seen it before."

"Jacob Marling's painting of the state house? Are you sure?"

"No. I'm not sure about anything! But it seems familiar somehow."

"The portal has to be the George Washington painting at the State Capitol," she said.

"You really think it could be my way home?" Daniel asked.

"I think there's a good chance."

She slapped the computer shut. "There's only one way to find out."

"How?" he asked.

"Get dressed," she said. "I have a plan! We're going to the State Capitol in downtown Raleigh to find the George Washington painting."

# CHAPTER
# THIRTY

*Daniel*

As soon as Abigail's mother dropped them off on Wilmington Street in front of the State Capitol, Daniel's stomach dropped. He was feeling all-overish uncomfortable. It was as if he had been there before but was unable to access the memory. A shudder ran down his spine.

The large, three-story building, built of massive squares of granite, shimmered underneath blue skies and a bright sun. It sat in the center of a large square of land full of tall trees, brick pathways, and metal benches. The building had a center colonnade with four Greek pillars that jutted out in the front. Two wings extended out from there, one on each side. It was very similar to the old Capitol in the Jacob Marling painting that had burned down in 1831.

"What's the next part of this plan of yours?" he asked, feeling like the earth beneath his feet was on a slight tilt.

"We're going to find the painting and see if anything comes to you."

"I wouldn't count on it."

Abigail sighed and picked up her pace.

They walked up the red brick pathway and stopped at a bronze statue of three U.S. presidents elevated on a platform of thick granite. The granite had been engraved with their names and the dates of their 1800s presidencies. James Polk and Andrew Johnson were seated, and Andrew Jackson towered above them on top of a large, bridled horse. All three were dressed finely in long formal coats, vests, and neckwear befitting a president.

"James Polk, Andrew Jackson..." Daniel read. A sparrow landed on Andrew Jackson's head and called out what sounded like an ominous warning.

Abigail pointed to the middle engraving. "Look, Andrew Jackson was president in 1831 when the Capitol burned down. He was born in North Carolina." She looked over at Daniel with hopeful eyes.

He shook his head. "I know he was a president, but I can't remember him being *my* president."

"Come on," she said.

Three stories of vacant windows loomed in front of them. Daniel rubbed his sweaty palms on his new jeans.

*My way home could be in this building.*

They followed a family towing two young children to the entrance. A quick check through security and a welcome by the front desk, and they were walking toward the rotunda with an NC State Capitol pamphlet in hand. Daniel stuffed his in his pocket. Abigail unfolded hers and read as they walked. He couldn't shake the uneasy feeling that the place held a mystery that it wanted to keep hidden. He reached in his back pocket and pulled out the red book. Holding it in his hand eased his fears.

They shuffled across the aged stone floors and arrived in the rotunda where a marble statue of George Washington sat atop a large pedestal of red granite. His attire consisted of a Roman military kilt, tightly fitted body armor, and sandals. The outfit wasn't too far off from the attire of the Israelite messenger in Egypt. George balanced an enormous tablet on one knee with his left hand, and in his right hand he held a pen. Something was carved on the tablet that Daniel couldn't read except for the name at the top—Giorgio Washington.

"It's Italian," Abigail said, reading her pamphlet. "The original artist, Antonio Canova, was Italian."

"So...George Washington is in Roman garb, writing Italian, but he was the first U.S. president."

Abigail chuckled. "That's art for you."

He scratched his head and looked up at the huge architectural dome above them. At its peak, blue sky shimmered through the glass that was framed like a wagon wheel. His head swam and a strange feeling consumed him—like he and Abigail weren't alone. The dome burst into flames and voices surrounded him.

*Stop!*

*Everyone get out!*

*Daniel...*

Was someone calling his name?

A hand touched his shoulder. He blinked and the vision was gone. A girl was standing there staring at him, and for just a brief second, he didn't know who she was.

"Abigail?" he asked.

"You were somewhere else. Where were you?"

"Nowhere." He should have told her what had just

happened, but he was scared. Something was off here. *He was off.*

"We should go find the George Washington painting by Thomas Sully," Abigail said. "The original statue of George Washington was destroyed in the 1831 fire, so I don't think this Roman slash Italian version of George is going to help you."

"Even if the painting is my way home, I don't know the portal password. There's not one in the book."

Abigail ignored him and examined her brochure. "It says it hangs in the House Chamber. That's on the second floor."

She skirted around Giorgio, and Daniel followed her down the hall and up a staircase. They came out in a circular rotunda that overlooked the George Washington statue below. Daniel avoided looking up or down.

"Over here is the House of Representatives," Abigail said, pushing on.

But then the voices came again—stronger this time —closer.

*"Come on! It's too late to save it!"*

*Smoke. So much smoke.*

Daniel struggled to breathe. A nonexistent smoke was filling his lungs.

"Daniel!" Abigail cried, "what's wrong with you?"

His breathing returned to normal. The voices fizzled into static, then disappeared.

Abigail glared at him. "Do you want to go home or not?"

He nodded, but his heart was racing, beating frantically against his ribs. He rubbed the spot in the middle of his chest. It hurt.

*What's happening to me?*

Abigail mumbled under her breath as she followed the brass railings and headed toward the tall, honey-colored doors that led to the former House of Representatives.

Daniel wanted to explain why he was acting so strangely, but something was holding him back. Maybe it was because he didn't understand what was happening himself.

He heard Abigail say, "Oh no."

"What's wrong?" he asked stepping in behind her. The room was in disrepair. There were a multitude of desks shoved in there, as if the room were being used for storage. It took him a moment to realize what the problem was.

Abigail pointed past the jumbled mess of desks to the end of the room where four white columns stood alongside a wooden podium. The wall behind was empty.

"The painting of George Washington isn't here!" She frantically fumbled with her visitor's brochure. "It says right here it hangs in the House."

There was a sign off to the left. "Look!" Daniel said. "The sign says they're doing restoration work. They must have removed the painting."

Abigail took a deep breath and let it out slowly. "Okay. No need to panic. We'll just go downstairs and find out where the painting is. It's probably in another room." She took off in a flash, leaving him behind.

He looked around the still, quiet room. Footsteps echoed from the balcony above him—then the distinct rattle of keys. Chills ran down his arms.

He slowly looked up. No one was there.

A woman screamed loud and long—a mournful wail.

The room suddenly turned hot. Something was wrong.

*"Fire! Fire!"*

Voices echoed in his head. He turned in circles looking for the voices, the fire. His head swam; his vision blurred.

*"Everybody out! Now!"*

"Who are you?" he yelled to the ceiling.

"Daniel!" Abigail barked.

He spun around. The feeling, the voices, all vanished.

"What's wrong with you?" Abigail asked. "You've been acting weird ever since we got here."

He wiped the sweat off his forehead with his arm. "Something's wrong here."

"Yeah," she huffed, "the painting is missing!"

He shook his head. "No, not that. Something else."

Abigail scanned the room. "What else?"

He couldn't keep this hidden from her. "I don't know how to explain it," he said.

She took a serious look at him. "You're shaking," she said, her eyes narrowing with concern. "Are you okay? I'm sorry, I got caught up in—"

"This place is speaking to me." He blurted it out.

Abigail's forehead creased. "What do you mean, it's speaking to you?"

"I can feel things, hear things," he whispered.

She scanned the room, as if she would find the source of his fear.

"It's like I have one foot in this time, and one foot in another."

Her eyes widened. "We have to find that painting and fast."

He nodded.

She took his hand. "We're in this together, okay?"

He squeezed her hand. "I couldn't have gotten this far without you."

She smiled, but it was a sad smile. They both knew that once he did get back home, they'd never see each other again.

They hurried down the stairs and made their way to the reception desk.

Abigail forcefully pushed her way in front of an elderly couple that was chatting about the weather with the lady at the desk.

"Where's the Sully painting of George Washington?" Abigail snapped.

The lady ignored Abigail and smiled at the older couple. "Enjoy your visit." The man and woman shuffled off, whispering about the rudeness of the current generation.

The receptionist's smile disappeared. "We're under an extensive renovation. The painting has been removed to prevent any possible damage."

"Then where is it?!"

The receptionist turned away and welcomed a middle-aged woman and a young man who by appearances was likely her son. "Welcome to the State Capitol." She handed them brochures, explained there was a renovation going on, and the pair moved on with amused grins.

"Miss!" Abigail protested. "Where is—"

Daniel pushed Abigail aside. "I apologize for the rudeness of my friend." He smiled.

The lady looked at Daniel over her glasses.

"What I believe she really meant to say is that we were very much looking forward to seeing the painting. When do you expect it to return?"

"Six months, maybe more."

Daniel's face flushed. *Six months!* A sick feeling formed deep in his gut.

"I'm sorry," the lady added. "It was moved to the NC Museum of Art a few weeks ago for safe storage."

He and Abigail looked at each other with wide eyes.

"Who do we know at the museum?" Abigail asked, smiling.

"Capability Brown," they said in unison.

# CHAPTER
# THIRTY-ONE

*Abigail*

"Let me get this straight," Cap said. "You have been using time portals at the museum to try and find a way home for Daniel, but that hasn't worked, so you want me to sneak you into a secure area of the art museum so you can find a painting of George Washington that's being stored for the NC State Capitol, so that Daniel here can see if it's a portal to the past because he's not from the 21$^{st}$ century." Cap took a deep breath.

"That's pretty much it, yes," Abigail said.

It did sound a bit ridiculous when said out loud. Daniel gave her an uncertain look. Maybe ambushing Cap on his way to his car in the museum parking lot hadn't been the best plan. But the sun was getting lower in the sky and the museum was about to close.

"If you had stuck around after Egypt and explained your

179

situation," Cap said with a scowl, "perhaps I'd be more inclined to help."

"Would you have believed us?" Abigail asked.

Cap rubbed the back of his neck. "If I hadn't experienced it for myself, I'd never have believed time travel was possible. Yet...theoretically, time travel *is* possible."

"How?" Daniel asked. "Because none of what has happened to me makes any sense. It's impossible!"

"Except it's not," Cap explained. "Many believe there are time portals hidden in our earth's magnetic fields." He pointed to the ground. "This land, here, where we're standing right now...it has a strange past."

"What kind of past?" Abigail asked.

"Native Americans once lived here. Then it was a civil war training site, then a youth prison. History exists all around you if you know what to look for."

She and Daniel shared a surprised look.

Cap continued. "NASA calls time portals Boom Tubes, but so far they've only acknowledged that they exist above earth."

"How do you know this stuff?" she asked.

"I have hobbies," Cap said, narrowing his eyes.

"What's nah-suh?" Daniel asked.

"Will you help us, Cap?" she begged, ignoring Daniel's question.

Cap put his hands on his hips and looked away, his jaw clenching.

Abigail didn't want to think of what would happen if Cap didn't help them. Daniel's strange experience at the Capitol building had to be a sign. The past hung in the balance—it was calling him home. She didn't know why, but she had an uneasy feeling that if he didn't go soon, he would be stuck in her time forever. He'd never know who he really was.

"Listen," Daniel said, breaking the silence. "I know it's a lot to ask, but you're my only hope. I'm sorry about the whole Egypt thing. We didn't mean to take you to Ancient Egypt, and we should have explained everything to you when we got back to the museum. We're sorry."

Cap slowly shook his head and chuckled. Abigail knew Cap was probably having a hard time processing what had happened and what they were asking him to do. But they needed him. His involvement in their plan was crucial. Finally, he sighed. "I can't believe I'm going to say this, but...okay. I'll help you. I can't pass up a chance like this. I need to know if time portals really do exist and that I didn't just imagine Ancient Egypt."

Abigail rushed into his arms, startling him. He stumbled back a bit before recovering himself.

"Yeah, okay," he said gently pushing her away. "No need for that. I haven't done anything. *Yet.*"

She and Daniel grinned at each other.

"We're going to do this my way, no questions asked," Cap said looking at Daniel. They both nodded. "Good," he said rubbing his hands together. "Not many get to see what you're about to see."

"What are we about to see?" Daniel asked.

"The art museum's vault."

# CHAPTER
# THIRTY-TWO

*Daniel*

A bigail bubbled with excitement as Cap ranted about portal-based time travel. Daniel, however, found it hard to put all his confidence in Cap. So far it had been just him and Abigail against the world. Now they had to rely on someone who ate things called jalapeño poppers and mumbled about electron diffusion regions and X-points. Daniel should have been grateful, but instead he found himself moping two steps behind them.

"Fascinating," Abigail said to one of Cap's long boring explanations about energy.

None of it meant anything to Daniel. Was it possible to be homesick when you didn't even know where home was? He wanted to believe he had a loving family waiting for him, but what if he didn't? Questions swirled in his head—too many questions. His temples throbbed.

Abigail must have sensed something was wrong. She stopped and slipped a hand under his elbow. "Are you okay?"

"Fine," he said, gently pushing her away.

She stared at him, motionless, a small look of surprised hurt on her face. Cap being Cap, told them to hurry up, that he didn't have all day. Daniel jogged to catch up, leaving Abigail behind for once.

They followed Cap into the East Building and down the stairs. An announcement blared over the intercoms that the museum would be closing in fifteen minutes. Cap ushered them into a back elevator closed off to the public. Daniel had watched people at the museum get into the strange contraption before, but he'd never dared venture into one. He swallowed his uneasy feeling.

"Ladies and gentlemen," Cap said, pressing a button. "You're about to enter the basement where the museum's vault resides. Please keep your hands to yourself and stay by my side at all times."

When the elevator *thunked* and the doors opened, a waft of cool air hit them as they stepped out into a hall of concrete— walls, floors, and ceiling. Florescent lights hummed from above. It was as if they had time traveled inside the museum and entered a secret bunker hidden from human eyes. Daniel wondered if he was about to go home or if this was going to be another dead end.

Their steps echoed down the hall as they approached huge, double metal doors. Cap entered a security code on a wall pad. The latches clicked and the doors swung open. A blast of icy air swept over them, blowing Daniel's hair back from his face. Lights flickered overhead and lit up the art vault.

The center of the vast room was lined with dozens of wooden panels on rollers. Some held ornate framed masterpieces, others held unframed canvases and small framed portraits. Against the walls of the room were hundreds of cage-like panels loaded with artwork that could be pulled in and out of their nesting places.

"Wow," Abigail whispered.

"Remember, no touching," Cap reminded them.

Sweat broke out on Daniel's forehead. The visions at the State Capitol had frightened him. Would the George Washington portrait bring on more? Abigail tried to take his hand, but he refused her.

*What is wrong with me?*

She had been more than a friend to him—she'd been like family.

Cap rubbed his hands together as they walked toward the back of the silent room. "Old George has been hanging in the State Capitol since 1818, except when it was saved from the fire," Cap said.

"You know about the fire?" Daniel asked.

"Yep. I know the State Capitol history. They say people hear things there sometimes."

A chill ran down Daniel's spine. "What kind of things?"

"Books falling off the shelves in the library on the second floor, doors closing in the middle of the night. Or distant singing, like a radio turned down low."

Abigail glanced over at Daniel, but he avoided eye contact.

"Ahhh. Here we are," Cap said.

Cap pressed a knob with his foot at the base of one of the metal panels, grabbed a handle attached to the side, and pulled the panel out toward them. The metal wall must have been ten feet long, and several paintings hung on the grate structure. Cap had only pulled out a few feet of panel before the life-sized painting of George Washington slid into view.

Daniel's heart pounded. There was something familiar. Some distant memory he couldn't access.

"Funny little story," Cap said. "This painting of George, or Giorgio as he's sometimes called at the Capitol, is a copy of a painting by another artist that hangs in the White House in Washington, DC. Dolly Madison saved it from a fire in 1814 when the white house burned down. What a strange coincidence, don't you think? Both paintings, identical, saved from fires in the same century."

"Yes, it is strange," Daniel said, studying the painting. George Washington was as lifelike as if he were standing there himself. His long black coat was rich velvet with a white ruffled shirt underneath and black tights below. His shoes were black with large silver buckles. Like the commander he was, he held a sword in his left hand and held out his right hand over an ornate, gold table, loosely covered with a thick, red cloth. On top of the table lay several items—a white-feathered pen sticking out of a silver ink well, a pair of books, parchment paper, and Washington's black hat. His right hand hovered above his pen, as if he were purposely drawing attention to his writing.

"Wow," Abigail said. She moved closer and peered down at the other paintings hanging past George.

"Not many people can say they've seen this particular painting up *this* close. It's hung in the State Capitol for over two hundred years," Cap said with pride.

Daniel's breathing became labored.

*What is this painting to me?*

His body felt heavy. A voice called to him.

*"Daniel!"*

But it was faint; he could scarcely hear it. He was so caught up in the painting, he hadn't realized that Abigail was calling his name—loudly. He blinked. She was pulling on the cage wall, trying to get it to come farther out.

"Hey!" Cap cried, putting out a hand to stop her, but she

185

pulled with all her might, and the steel wall squeaked out. There must have been a dozen additional framed paintings hanging there, all various sizes.

"Daniel," Abigail whispered, pointing to a picture hung high.

It was a portrait of a pale boy with light brown hair and blue eyes. The clothes were from another century—formal, black jacket; big, collared white shirt; gold vest. If it hadn't been for the book in the portrait, Daniel might have glanced over it. But this wasn't just a painting of a boy. It was a younger version of *himself* holding the red book!

"Well, I'll be," Cap said. "Cut your hair and shave off a few years, and this is definitely you."

Daniel's face grew hot, the room disappeared. He felt himself falling.

CHAPTER

# THIRTY-THREE

*Abigail*

"Daniel!" Abigail patted Daniel's cheek. "Daniel, wake up." Cap stood above her, rubbing his hands together. "Could you get him some water?" Abigail asked.

"Water? Look around you. There's no water down here."

She sighed. "Then help me sit him up."

Cap crouched down beside her and lifted Daniel's shoulders into her lap. She smoothed back his shaggy brown hair away from his face. "Daniel," she said softly.

Cap paced in front of them.

Daniel blinked.

"That's it," she said, continuing to stroke his hair. "Come back to us."

Daniel opened his eyes wide and jumped up like an animal freed from a trap. He immediately returned to the painting of

187

himself. He stood motionless, breathing heavily. She placed a hand on his back. This time he didn't push her away.

"Tell me about this painting," Daniel said, without looking at Cap.

"Well...it's called *The Unknown Boy*."

Daniel clasped a hand to his mouth. Abigail wrapped an arm around his shoulders.

"It was painted by Jacob Marling," Cap added.

Stunned, Abigail turned to Cap. "Are you sure?"

Cap nodded. "Sure as I'm standing here."

"Daniel, this has to mean something," she said with excitement. "Maybe that's why you recognized the watercolor painting of the old State Capitol by Jacob Marling. You know him because he painted a portrait of you!"

Daniel slowly removed the red book from his back pocket. He held it up near the painting.

"It's the same book!" Abigail said.

"I don't understand," Daniel said. "Why would Jacob Marling paint a picture of me?"

"And the clothes, Daniel," she said, ignoring his question and pointing at the painting. "No orphan would wear those kind of clothes."

He nodded, but his eyes looked troubled.

Abigail was sure that the fine clothes Daniel was wearing in the painting meant that he had a family, or at least some relative with the means to pay for a portrait.

She side-stepped over to the Washington painting. Daniel joined her in front of the grand picture, and they studied it together.

"The fact that your picture is hanging near this one can't be a coincidence," Abigail said. "It has to be a sign. The Washington painting has to be your way home."

"We don't have a password," Daniel reminded her.

"Password?" Cap asked.

"Like the one we used to get to Egypt and back," Abigail said.

"Oh, like, '*May we find the favor of him who dwelt in the burning bush*'?"

"Exactly."

"Hmmm," Cap murmured, scratching his chin.

"None of this is going to matter if we can't figure out what the password is for this painting," Daniel murmured.

"If it were me," Cap said, "I'd put the clue in the painting."

All three of them huddled around the painting and studied it. After a few moments of silence Daniel spoke. "I'm never getting back."

Abigail touched his arm. "Don't say that. We're going to figure it out." Daniel had been through so much, maybe he had given up without even realizing it

"Look at Washington's hand," Cap said. "It looks like he's calling attention to his pen."

"Yes. So?" Daniel said glumly.

"Maybe it's something Washington has written."

"Yes!" Abigail said shaking Daniel a little. "It's worth a try."

"Really?" Daniel asked. "Are we to recite everything he's ever written?"

"No," Cap said, his eyes alight with excitement. "What's at the Capitol that George Washington has written?" Daniel and Abigail stared at Cap. Cap spread his arms open. "His farewell address!"

"What farewell address?" Daniel asked.

Cap sighed and placed his large hand on Daniel's shoulder.

"Washington's statue in the State Capitol rotunda," Abigail said. "He's writing to the states to announce his decision not to run for president again."

"Bingo!" Cap said, clapping his hands together.

"But it's written in Italian," Daniel pointed out.

Cap smiled his big, white smile that shined right through his big, brown eyes. "Lucky for you, I know what it says in English."

Abigail wanted to shout for joy. Could this be the answer they were looking for? It was a long shot, but that was more than they had a few minutes ago.

Cap belted out, "To the People of the United States—1796 —Friends and Citizens."

As soon as the words were out of his mouth, Abigail's vision blurred. She fell through time, spinning, swimming. But this time was different. Fire and smoke swirled around her, yet she didn't burn. Voices hissed at her in hurried whispers.

*Fire!*

*Everyone out!*

*Fire!*

# THIRTY-FOUR

*Jacob Marling – NC painter*
*June 21, 1831*
*Raleigh, NC*

M arling held his cards in one hand and pulled his pocket watch from his vest with the other—4:00 a.m.

A vague promise of light broke through the tall front windows of his friend's parlor. Jacob and his card playing friends had lost track of time in their pursuit of merriment. Mrs. Marling would surely have words with him when he returned home. But Jacob would compliment the delicate way she served morning tea, ask her how her latest painting was progressing, tend to the chores he'd left undone, and by noon she would have forgiven his late night. Thus was the way of his fair wife. Never was there a woman with a more forgiving nature than Louisa.

Marling laid down his cards. "Gentlemen," he said, rising. "I must leave. Mrs. Marling will be preparing breakfast soon."

There were moans and pleas from the other men, begging him to stay. He held up a hand in protest and gathered his hat. The other men threw in their cards, which put an end to their long night.

"Next Monday? Same time?" Marling asked. There were grunts of agreement as the other men rose and wearily collected jackets and hats.

Satisfied that plans had been confirmed for next week, he thanked his host and let himself out the front door. He paused briefly on the stately front porch with its large white columns. A light fog had blanketed the city. He placed his hat on his head and considered his next move. He could turn right and go home, or he could go left and check on the progress being made on fireproofing the State Capitol's roof. The workers would start early to avoid the afternoon heat.

Louisa would likely still be sleeping, so he turned left and headed toward the town square. He had not heard from Daniel. The boy was quite good at disappearing when he wanted to. Marling's messages had gone unanswered. If he didn't hear from Daniel today, he'd have to go searching for him. The boy had been quite taken with the red book, now that he thought about it. Pleased with Daniel's curiosity, Marling had given it to him on a whim while painting his portrait a few years ago. The book had been full of strange words—references to time travel and art that didn't exist. The small volume had been just one of many sorts of oddities Marling had kept from the North Carolina museum he'd started in Raleigh several years ago—maps, rare coins, literary works, art, the strange and the unusual. But Marling and Company was no more, and neither was the museum.

If he remembered correctly, the book had been one of many dusty relics contained in a box donated to his museum. To have been asked to return the book now, after all this time, was strange, but he dared not deny the request. The museum was a thing of the past, and the owner had every right to ask for its return.

He glided through the fog, only to find himself pausing on the sidewalk to greet the chubby-cheeked face of a man affectionately known to the locals as Whisker. His small black dog was in tow, digging his nose into the grass. Whisker worked at the newspaper—The Raleigh Times. Early mornings were commonplace for journalists eager to meet a new day of fresh inspiration and news.

"Good morning, Mr. Marling. Quite early for a morning stroll, wouldn't you say? And a devil of a fog," Whisker said in his gristly tone. The dog, having satisfied his tameless curiosity, wagged his tail in a very lively manner and pulled at his owner's leash in order to smell Marling's leg.

Jacob responded with a friendly pat on the eager dog's head. "Quite in agreement, Whisker," he replied.

Whisker shifted his weight to his right leg—for the man had a stout belly. "There's definitely something strange in the air this morning. I can feel it in my aching bones."

"Indeed," Marling said. "How goes the news business?"

"Eh," Whiskers said with an air of boredom. "Nothing much to report."

"Sorry to hear it."

"Say," Whiskers said, looking over his shoulder toward his house. "How about a tea to start your day? I'd love to hear whose portrait you're painting these days. You'll be running out of customers soon at the rate you're going."

Marling smiled graciously. A bit of polite conversation over tea was a courtesy he never refused. Besides, it was still very early. He had plenty of time before his day really began. "I'd love to."

# THIRTY-FIVE

*Daniel*

Daniel held his breath as he fell though time. Slowly, almost imperceptibly, his memories returned one by one while he swirled in the dark abyss.

*I know who I am. I remember!*

Before he'd even gained full awareness of his surroundings, he was screaming. "I know who I am!"

As soon as his vision cleared, he spun in circles, taking in the State Capitol, the green grass, the trees, the dampness that summer carried with it in the mornings. All at once he was full and complete. The familiar clamor of horse and carriage was like breathing fresh air. He was no longer in Abigail's time. He was in his—1831.

A man in rugged pants and a stained shirt moist with sweat walked past, a leather tool belt strapped around his waist.

"Excuse me, sir. What day is it?"

"Tuesday," the man growled and marched on.

"Um...Daniel."

*Abigail?*

He turned to find Abigail and Cap standing directly behind him. He grabbed Abigail by the shoulders. "I remember! I remember everything! I have a mother and father, a baby sister. My dad owns the stationer store on Fayetteville Street."

Abigail gave him a polite smile.

His stomach dropped. "Oh," he said, releasing her.

"Oh, is right," she said, looking around.

"I guess the password worked," Cap said sheepishly.

Daniel pulled at his hair.

Abigail reached out and gave him a light touch on the arm. "It's okay. We'll get back—without you this time."

She smiled, but there was the same sadness in her eyes that he felt every time he thought of never seeing her again.

Daniel glanced at the Capitol. "Well, the Capitol building is still standing, so it hasn't burned down yet. We just have to go in and find the George Washington painting and you two..." He trailed off when he realized three things:

One, he'd been *in* the Capitol at the time the fire started and had murmured many ridiculous phrases in front of the George Washington painting, trying to unlock the red book's time travel claim. Two, the Capitol was still standing, which meant he'd come back slightly sooner than the fire, and it wasn't too late to stop it. Third, most Black people were not free in 1831. They were slaves. Many had helped build the Capitol. He looked gingerly at Cap.

Cap rubbed his hands together and scanned the Capitol grounds.

Daniel's face flushed with heat. "Cap—"

Cap held up a hand. "No need to explain. I know my history."

"I want you to know that my family doesn't think it's right. We don't have any..."

"Let's just get this over with before someone starts asking questions we can't answer," Cap said.

Daniel nodded.

"Fire!" someone screamed out.

"No," Daniel said, searching the Capitol roof.

Abigail pointed. "There."

Sure enough, a small amount of smoke was streaming from the roof near the dome. Daniel gritted his teeth. Shouts of "fire" echoed across the lawn as more and more people came out of their homes and businesses and saw the smoke. Men and women, many of whom were still wearing their bed clothes, ran toward the Capitol, yelling for water and buckets.

"Great," Cap said. "The painting is inside."

"We have to make sure they save it," Daniel said.

The people of Raleigh were quickly forming lines, readying to pass buckets of water. The three of them hurried toward the closest entrance. They crossed paths with a group of men struggling to push a fire hand pump.

"You," one of them shouted, pointing at Cap. "Help us."

The three of them froze. "He's with us," Daniel said. "We're getting water buckets." He hated lying, but he wouldn't abandon Cap. Besides, Daniel already knew from history that the efforts to stop the fire would fail. The men scowled but pushed on with grunts and groans.

"That was close," Cap said, wiping his brow with his short sleeve.

Shouts and screams came from all around them. By the time they reached the side door, large billows of smoke were already rolling off the roof and pouring into the square. The treetops swayed with a light breeze. If the wind carried away embers, the whole city could go up in flames.

Daniel prayed that everything would go as history had already recorded it. He and Abigail had changed bits of history in France and Egypt, even though they had tried not to. But this...this was his time, his life.

They climbed the steps to the large double doors. Cap pulled at the door. "It's locked," he said. "Now what?"

Daniel's heart pounded, and the three of them stared at each other breathlessly. The sky darkened with smoke.

"Daniel!" A man ran toward them.

Daniel hurried down the steps to meet him. "Mr. Marling!"

Breathless, Jacob Marling handed him a large key. Then from around the corner, a mass of people with wooden buckets hurried toward them, sloshing water about their feet. Without a word, Daniel took the key and ran back up the steps and handed it to Cap who took it and inserted it into the large keyhole. With a single turn, the cylinders of the lock clicked. Cap pulled the large doors open one at a time. A small wisp of smoke escaped.

The hall was hazy, but the fire hadn't yet reached the first floor. They waited until the men with buckets filed inside and then followed close behind. The bucket brigade took to the stairs. Daniel, Abigail, and Cap ran down the hall to the rotunda where the marble statue of George Washington stood. There were already close to twenty men surrounding the statue, all working to save it. The men grunted as they tried to shove multiple crowbars underneath the statue's base. A blanket of fire had covered the dome above them, glowing a bright yellow. They didn't have much time. If that dome collapsed, everyone below it would die.

"We need to find that painting," Cap said, holding his arm up to his nose.

There was commotion at the other end of the hall.

"Down there!" Daniel shouted.

As they passed the men working to save the statue, one of them grabbed Cap and pulled him into the group trying to push the statue on its side.

"Cap!" Abigail cried.

"Go!" Cap said. "Go!" Then Cap dug his large shoulder into the base of the statue, and all the men heaved with grunts and shouts.

Daniel hesitated.

"Come on," Abigail said, pulling at Daniel's arm. "If we don't make sure that painting is saved, Cap and I may never get home."

"You're right," he said, pulling himself together.

They ran down the opposite hall. Men and women were scrambling out of offices with arms full of papers and leather-bound books. Orders were shouted out, what to save, what to leave. He and Abigail were barely noticed. They checked two or three rooms, but the Washington painting was nowhere to be seen. Had someone already saved it? He could have sworn it was in one of these rooms, but in all the confusion, he was having a hard time getting his bearings.

The smoke grew denser. Each breath became more difficult as his lungs filled with smoke. They didn't have much time.

"Daniel!" someone shouted.

They turned to find Jacob Marling headed their way.

"You two need to get out of here. It's not safe."

"The painting," Daniel said. "We have to save the painting of George Washington."

"The statue is more important."

"No!" Daniel yelled. "It's not!"

Mr. Marling pulled a handkerchief from his breast pocket and held it to his nose.

"Mr. Marling, please!"

Screams erupted from the rotunda, followed by a large crash. The three of them ran back to the rotunda. A huge chunk of ceiling had fallen, and two men were pinned under the partially burning rubble.

"Cap!" Abigail shouted. They both searched the room, looking for him.

Shouts came for water. Several men with buckets came running and doused the flames of the rubble, and the two men were pulled from underneath it.

Neither of the men were Cap.

Daniel and Abigail looked up. The fire had spread beyond the dome and was now a growing, churning blanket of blue and yellow flames. They had only minutes, before the whole ceiling collapsed into the rotunda.

"It's too late!" Daniel yelled. "The statue can't be saved!"

"Save the George Washington painting!" Mr. Marling yelled to the remaining men. "Hurry!"

The men hesitated at first, but after another loud crack from the ceiling, everyone hurried out of the way as another large piece fell from above. George Washington's arm holding the tablet snapped off and crashed to the ground.

*Where is Cap? This can't be happening.*

"You two, out of here. Now!" Marling shouted.

Daniel opened his mouth to protest, but by this time Abigail was bent over, coughing uncontrollably. He had to get her out of here.

"Follow me," Marling shouted to the men. With no time to spare, the men followed him.

Daniel put his arm around Abigail, and they stumbled through the smoke, past the last few people running about with papers and books. Suddenly, Daniel couldn't hear anymore. Shouts were whispers. Time stopped. He was walking through time as thick as mud. He could barely register a thought. He and Abigail tumbled out of the burning Capitol, staggered to safer ground, and collapsed on the grass, coughing.

"Are you okay?" he asked Abigail.

She nodded between coughs. He scooted over and put an arm around her shoulder.

*This is my fault. She shouldn't be here. Cap shouldn't be here.*

"Cap," Abigail gasped.

"I don't know what happened to him."

Had he been among the injured? In all the chaos, had they just missed him being pulled from the flaming rubble? Daniel stood up and offered Abigail a hand. Abigail took a few deep breaths and grabbed his hand.

Standing there watching the Capitol burn was a sight he'd never forget. Every window was full of flames. Dark, billowing smoke twirled and spiraled, forming a dark cloud above the city. The line of people who were passing buckets slowed as the fire overtook their efforts. Suddenly everyone stopped and stood still, gaping at the Capitol in disbelief. Buckets were dropped to the ground. Handkerchiefs came out, and the men wiped soot-stained brows. The citizens stared in disbelief, and children clung to their parent's legs.

A heartbreaking sob came out of Daniel's mouth. He took off running toward the building. "Cap! Cap!" He grabbed a full bucket that someone had set down.

"Daniel!" Abigail called after him.

A few people tried to reach out and stop him, but he shrugged them off.

*Cap can't be gone. He just can't.*

The doors were wide open. Smoke rolled out of the top of the doorframe. Flickers of flames danced at the windows, and the shattering of window glass sounded one after another like a symphony's grand finale. He ran inside without thinking.

"It's too late!" someone shouted.

He was surprised to find a handful of men still inside. But they were backing out. One tried pulling Daniel with him, but Daniel broke free only to be grabbed by another and dragged, kicking, toward the door. His bucket fell to the ground. Just as he was pulled to safety the entire domed ceiling collapsed on top of George Washington's statue, and it disappeared, buried in flames.

"Cap!" Daniel shouted one last time into the carnage. His rescuer dragged him outside.

Abigail took a hold of him, easing him back even farther.

"Abigail. No," he whispered.

Exhausted men and women sat on the lawn, caps in hand, stunned and weeping. The crew that had been working the fire hand pump stopped and stared at the flames bursting out of the windows from all floors.

The Capitol was lost.

Tears welled in Daniel's eyes. Cap was the reason he'd gotten home. Without him, he would have been stuck in the 21st century forever. He owed him his life. Abigail took him into her arms, and they held each other, not knowing what would come next.

Had the painting of George Washington been saved? Would Abigail have a way home, or was she stuck in 1831? Was Cap dead, never to return home? He closed his eyes and pulled Abigail closer to him, and she cried into his shoulder.

# CHAPTER
# THIRTY-SIX

*Daniel*

D aniel held Abigail's hand as they stood watching with a kind of numb shock as the flames took everything with an unquenchable appetite. Some stray embers carried by the morning breeze had caught a few nearby houses on fire, but those fires were quickly doused by the men with the fire pump. The city had been spared, but the Capitol was a complete loss, just like history had written it. Even though he'd known it was going to happen, nothing could have prepared him for this. Not Calais or Thebes.

People wandered the grounds, tired, weeping, and looking for loved ones. Cap was missing, probably dead. Daniel had no idea how Abigail was going to get back home. There was no sign of the George Washington painting, just the piles and piles of papers and books that were now stacked on the Capitol lawn.

Somewhere nearby, shouts of joy broke through the solemn moment.

*Who would celebrate at a time like this?*

He stood on his toes, peering over the crowds of people that had gathered to watch the fire. A large group marched around the corner, clapping and cheering. Was that...?

*No, it can't be.*

Everyone's attention turned. He tugged at Abigail's hand and pushed through the crowds.

"What's going on?" Abigail asked.

He wasn't sure what he'd seen, but his heart raced with hope. When they finally broke through the mass of people, there, standing in front of them, was Cap with a big smile on his face and a painting the size of a very large table lifted over his head. The people of Raleigh cheered and pushed in all around him, patting him on the back, jostling him about with their excitement. Then, to his surprise, the crowd applauded. Daniel and Abigail grinned at each other even as they were tousled about by the growing audience that was anxious to see the big man with the big painting.

Daniel and Abigail laughed and cried and let themselves become enveloped by the sweat and smoke and cheers of the men, women, and children of Raleigh. The celebration was short, for some small debris fires had ignited and many rushed off to help.

As soon as Cap put the painting down, Jacob Marling and a few others took it away to examine it for damage.

"Daniel! Abigail!" Cap shouted with arms spread wide.

"You could have gotten yourself killed," Abigail said with a small scowl on her face. But Daniel knew she was as relieved as he was.

Cap stuck his chest out and rubbed his belly. "They don't call me Capability Brown for nothing!"

Daniel laughed. Abigail tried to maintain her stern face but ended up bursting into laughter. The three of them drew together, and Cap wrapped his big arms around both of them. They got a few strange looks, but they didn't care. Daniel was home, Cap had saved the painting, and now Abigail and Cap could go home too. All had been set right. But in their excitement over Cap being alive and the painting saved, they'd failed to notice the woman standing right in front of them.

Abigail gasped. Daniel's celebratory smile quickly faded.

*The woman in black!*

Cap wiped a hand across his sweaty face and took a step toward the woman.

Daniel balled his hands into fists. "Leave us alone!"

Cap crossed his large arms and set his feet.

A muscle twitched in the woman's jaw. She held out her hand to Daniel for the book.

"I don't think so," Cap said. "It ends here, Maki."

"What's going on?" Abigail whispered urgently to Daniel.

Daniel shook his head.

The woman in black sneered. "I'm not afraid of you Capability. I never have been."

Abigail's mouth fell open. Daniel was just as stunned. *They know each other? How?*

"It ends here," Cap said. "The book belongs to the Order."

Maki approached with confidence, within a breath of Cap's face.

"I'd hate for your little friends to get hurt. You can't protect them forever."

"If you touch one hair on their heads—"

Maki smiled with amusement. "You'll what? Ban me from the Order? Oh wait," she said stepping back. "You already did that."

Daniel's whole body tensed. "Cap. What's going on?"

Daniel put a protective arm in front of Abigail and drove them both back a few steps.

"Yes, Capability. Why don't you tell these children what's going on?"

"We're teenagers!" Abigail blurted out.

Cap and Maki stared at each other in a battle of wills.

Maki finally cut her eyes to Daniel and Abigail. "Did he tell you he's from the future?"

"What?" Abigail and Daniel said in unison.

"Oh, he didn't?" Maki laughed. "Well, he always was a liar."

Daniel's stomach churned.

*He's been lying to us all this time?*

"He belongs to The Fantastic Order of Odd Travelers—time travelers from the future sworn to protect history."

Abigail and Daniel shared confused looks.

"Cap?" Daniel asked sadly. "Is this true?"

"Yes," he said gruffly. "I didn't tell you because the Order is secret. We've sworn an oath."

"Oath!" Daniel screamed. "What about us, huh? You made us trust you. You acted like a fool in Egypt, like you didn't know anything!"

Maki smirked. "He used you. Don't you see? He doesn't care about you."

"The book belongs to the Order," Cap said, keeping one eye on Maki. "It's our job to protect history."

Abigail slipped her hand under Daniel's arm.

Maki locked eyes with Abigail. "Wouldn't you change history if you could? Think of all the good you could do. What about your friend in Calais? Why should they have suffered such injustice? All that can be undone."

Abigail squeezed Daniel's arm. The woman's gaze was cold and hard.

"And what about Mery?" Maki continued, focusing on Daniel. "Her mother died so young. You could have saved—"

"Be quiet!" Daniel shouted.

"You can save her," Maki said, softening. "The Order would have us all suffer the worst."

Daniel took the book out of his pocket and looked at it like it was poison. He looked over at Abigail, unsure of what to do. Cap had lied to them. Maki's motives were questionable. There was no way to know who to trust, so there was only one thing to do. The red book needed to be destroyed.

"Wake *fire* snakes?" he asked Abigail, hoping she understood his meaning behind *fire*.

She nodded.

Cap took his eyes off Maki for the first time. "Wait just one minute you two."

"Wake..." Abigail said quietly.

"SNAKES!" Daniel shouted.

Then they both turned and sprinted straight toward the Capitol.

"Daniel!" Cap called out.

Daniel pulled ahead of Abigail. He could hear her coughing as she struggled to keep up. The smoke had taken its toll on her.

Cap yelled over and over for Daniel to stop.

"Run, Daniel! Run!" Abigail shouted between coughs.

Daniel glanced back to make sure she was okay, but Cap was sprinting straight for him, so he kept running. He had no idea if he and Abigail were doing the right thing.

He was almost within reach of the Capitol fire when Cap caught him from behind.

"No!" he heard Abigail scream.

Daniel kicked and struggled to hold the book out of Cap's reach while Cap held him off the ground with one arm and grasped for the book with his free hand. Abigail was still running, Maki on her heels. As soon as Abigail got close to Daniel, she held out her hands, and he tossed her the book. By some miracle, it landed in her smoked-stained fingers, and she continued running. The heat and smoke of the fire was intense, but she only needed to get close enough to throw.

Cap put Daniel down with a grunt but kept a hold of him. It was too late to stop Abigail now. Daniel held his breath as she pulled back her arm to throw the book into the fire. But just as she was about to release the book, Maki caught up and tackled her, and the book went flying out of Abigail's hand, falling just short of the Capitol's flames.

"Abigail!" Daniel cried, pulling against Cap's grip.

Daniel watched helplessly as Abigail tried to crawl toward the book, but Maki had hold of her ankle. Abigail stretched out her arm as far as it could go, reaching desperately for the book. She tried to kick her leg free. But Maki only bared her teeth and dragged Abigail farther and farther away from the book. Daniel's heart sank as Abigail clawed at the ash-covered ground with her fingers. She finally twisted her ankle free and tried to push herself to her feet, but Maki stomped a foot into her back, knocking her hard into the ground. Abigail lifted her head helplessly as Maki strode past her and snatched the red book off the ground.

*No!* Daniel reached out for the book as though he could will it to come to him.

"Stay here," Cap growled, releasing Daniel.

Daniel stood transfixed by Maki's triumphant face. He thought Cap was going after Maki, but instead, Cap stopped and lifted Abigail into his arms. That's when Daniel realized he'd lost sight of what really mattered to him. He ran to Abigail's side as another round of coughing wracked her whole body.

"Are you okay?" he asked, as he rubbed a hand across her forehead.

She nodded weakly.

Cap lowered her to the ground but kept a supporting arm around her shoulder.

In the midst of the billowing smoke with flames leaping behind her, Maki held the red book up and smiled.

Daniel took a step toward her, but Cap reached out and gently stopped him.

An ear shattering crack came from above as the glass in more Capitol windows shattered. Flames shot out of the second story along with a blast of glass shards.

Cap took several steps back with Abigail, urging Daniel with his other hand to follow.

"We have to stop her," Daniel pleaded.

"I've saved what matters, son," he said, looking over at Daniel with tender eyes. "You and Abigail."

Maki dusted the book off. "I've won, you see." An evil madness glowed in her eyes.

"No," Cap said calmly looking up at the roof of the Capitol, "you've lost."

Maki's face suddenly went cold with fear. She looked up just as a large chunk of building broke away and tumbled toward her. Maki dashed for safety, but it was too late. The flaming debris fell on top of her with a loud boom. Cap put his other arm around Daniel as the woman in black and the red book disappeared into a gulf of flames.

CHAPTER

# THIRTY-SEVEN

*Daniel*

The three of them sat on the lawn of the Capitol, tired and spent. The George Washington painting rested against a large oak, safe and sound, but Maki and the red book had not been so lucky. Daniel wasn't sure what had just happened. There were more questions than answers.

Cap rubbed his hands together, shut his eyes, and licked his lips. "I belong to the Fantastic Order of Odd Travelers," he said, opening his eyes.

Daniel and Abigail exchanged tentative looks. Could they really trust anything Cap said?

"We...the Order, guard earth's portals and make sure history stays intact."

"How do we know you're telling the truth?" Daniel asked.

"And that you're who you say you are?" Abigail added.

"How did I know the password for the George Washington painting?"

"Lucky guess?" Daniel suggested.

"And the Pharaoh's snake god amulet in Egypt. Why do you think I pointed it out to you?"

Daniel shrugged.

"I needed to get you two back to the museum before you changed more of history."

An uncomfortable knot formed in Daniel's throat. Abigail opened her mouth, but no words came out. Daniel was equally as speechless.

"I'm from the future. I give you my word," Cap said, looking back and forth between them.

"Promise us you're not lying," Abigail snapped.

Cap placed both hands over his heart.

*How had they missed this?*

"But you were surprised and confused in Egypt," Daniel said. "You acted like a complete idiot!"

"The Order is a secret. So, you know...I'm supposed to stay secret. I did what I could to help you without giving myself away."

Daniel shook his head in disbelief. Cap *had* been the one to point out Necho's amulet. It was all starting to make sense.

"Then why did your Odd Fantastic Traveler people let Daniel go through all those portals?" Abigail asked. "Why didn't you stop him?"

Cap scratched the back of his head. "The museum portals haven't been used in a very long time. It took us a while to realize someone was traveling through them. Imagine our surprise to find a boy from 1831."

"So, these Fantastic Odd Traveler people sent you here to what? Stop me?" Daniel asked.

"To protect you," Cap said, "It's not true what Maki said.

The Order cares about you. We needed you to go home. Believe it or not, we all have a part in history. Even you, Daniel."

Abigail reached for Daniel's hand. His temples began to pound. "So, the woman in black, Maki, was one of your people just trying to get the book back?" he asked.

"No longer one of us. She was banned from the Order. She's been hunting the missing book ever since. Who knows the damage she could have done by going back and changing history?"

"Then why didn't you just take the book from Daniel in Egypt?" Abigail asked.

"My job was to guide Daniel home safely first."

Daniel swallowed. It was true that without Cap, Daniel would have never gotten home. That had to mean something.

"How was Maki able to follow us back in time?" Abigail asked.

"It's hard to explain. It's simpler just to say she piggy-backed on your jumps."

"We took her right through the portals," Daniel said.

Cap nodded. "It's okay. You didn't know. Look, I've already said too much. You just need to know that the Fantastic Order of Odd Travelers works for the good of all earth. History must be preserved. I promise you two, we're the good guys here."

"What about what Maki said about going back and changing history so those bad things don't happen?" Daniel asked.

Cap smiled. "The one thing we can't change is the evil that comes out of a man's heart. Every injustice that could be undone would only lead to more injustices. The loop of undoing history would be endless."

Somehow that made sense to Daniel. Even if the Order managed to change one horrible moment in the course of history, more would follow.

"How does it all turn out?" Abigail asked. "You know, in the future."

Cap smiled his big white smile. "It's still being written."

Daniel's fears subsided. "I'm sorry about the book. If I had known, I wouldn't have tried to throw it in the fire."

Cap stood up and brushed himself off. "It's probably for the best. Now the red book can't fall into the wrong hands."

Daniel helped Abigail up.

"I'm counting on you two to keep the Order a secret."

They both nodded.

"We need to go, Abigail," Cap said. "I'm not exactly a free man here. It won't be long before someone starts asking questions." Cap grinned and shook Daniel's hand, and then left him alone with Abigail so they could say their goodbyes.

Daniel stood motionless, unable to grasp that he would never see Abigail again. She had become a true friend.

"I didn't expect things to end like this. So...suddenly," Abigail said.

"I know. I wish we had more time."

His throat swelled with emotion. With all the commotion of the fire, he hadn't had a chance to even tell her his last name. Daniel smiled. "By the way, my last name is Truly. My name is Daniel Truly."

She laughed a little and a tear rolled down her face. "I'm happy you're home now Daniel Truly. And that you have a family and—"

He took her hand and held it gently. "I wouldn't have gotten home without you and Cap. All that time I thought the book would save me, but it was my friends..." His throat swelled with emotion.

"It's our friends that we can really count on." She sniffed, squeezing his hand.

"Our great adventure is over," he said with a weak smile.

"Abigail!" Cap called out, motioning her over.

Daniel pulled Abigail into an embrace, and they held each other so tightly that it hurt. Somehow, she had become his life raft, and he had become hers.

"You'll always be the best friend I ever had," she whispered.

"And you'll always be mine, Abigail Hawk."

Daniel released her and she turned and ran to Cap, straight into his big arms. Tears were running down her face.

As luck would have it, Marling had stepped away from the George Washington painting and was currently absorbed in a conversation with a plumpish man who was rapidly jotting down notes on a small pad.

Cap gave a final wave to Daniel.

*To the People of the United States—1796—Friends and Citizens.*

*Good-bye, Abigail.*

And just like that, in the blink of an eye, Cap and Abigail were gone.

CHAPTER
# THIRTY-EIGHT

*Abigail*

S omeone rapped lightly on Abigail's bedroom door. "Abigail?"

Abigail rolled over and looked at the clock on her bedside table—11:00 a.m. beamed bright and red. She sat up and dangled her bare feet off the side of the bed. "I'm up," she said, her voice like sandpaper.

"Would you like some breakfast? Or lunch?"

Was she hungry? Her stomach growled. "Sure. Be right down."

She reluctantly rose to her feet and stood in front of the full-length mirror hanging on the backside of her bedroom door. Her eyes were swollen and puffy, her hair a frizzy, tangled mess. She looked about how she felt.

She slipped her feet into her bunny ear slippers and dragged herself downstairs to the kitchen and stood by the kitchen table. Her mother pulled out a bagel from the toaster and slathered it with a gob of cream cheese—just the way Abigail liked it. Watching her mother do such a simple thing filled her with an overwhelming sense of gratitude.

*I have a family.*

It didn't matter that her family was broken and imperfect. She didn't have an army outside her city, or a Pharaoh taking her mother to war. She had a life that Jean de Fienne and Mery could have only dreamed of. Turning thirteen was beginning to feel like a new beginning instead of something to dread.

"You must have had some kind of birthday," her mother said.

Abigail dropped into a chair and watched as a finch pinched thistle seeds from the feeder hanging by the kitchen window. She took a deep breath through her nose and savored the smell of home—lingering vanilla candle, toasted bread.

"I guess between the museum and the Capitol, you and Daniel wore yourselves out."

"Something like that," she murmured, resting in the peacefulness of home.

"Well, I like Daniel," her mother said. "He seemed to be nice boy. Though I have to question why any parent in their right mind would leave a child alone while they left the country." Her mother set the bagel in front of Abigail along with a glass of juice. "Where does Daniel go to school? I should call the principal."

Abigail fingered the bagel. "His parents came back last night. They're moving to Egypt." Daniel would have liked that thumper. The old word for a telling a lie made her smile. She'd miss Daniel's quirky words.

"Egypt?" Her mom placed a hand on her shoulder. "Well, I'm sure you two will stay in touch."

Abigail stared at her juice. "Mom?"

"Yes, dear."

"My new school has a history club. I think I'm going to join. Maybe I can make some friends that way."

Her mother sat down across from her and smiled. "I think that sounds like a wonderful idea."

"They do field trips to historical sites, and you get to investigate different eras and stuff."

"I had no idea you were interested in history. I thought you were leaning toward art."

Abigail smiled. "Oh, I'm still interested in art. You have *no* idea how much the two are tied together."

Her mother patted Abigail's hand. "Then I'll look forward to your discoveries." Her mother stood and returned to the kitchen counter. "This came for you yesterday. Registered mail and everything."

Abigail lifted the bagel to her mouth and took a giant bite. "What is it?" she mumbled between chews.

Her mother raised an eyebrow as she held out the envelope. "I don't know, but it looks very old."

She reached out and plucked the tea-stained envelope from her mother's hand. It was addressed to her, but the handwriting was horrendous, barely legible.

*It can't be.*

She tried to swallow, but instead choked on her food. She coughed and coughed. Her mother hit her soundly on the back. Abigail grabbed her juice and gulped it down. After four swallows, she could breathe again.

"Thanks for the breakfast, Mom."

Abigail ran up the stairs into her bedroom and locked the door. She sat on the edge of her bed and stared at the envelope. Taking a deep breath, she opened the letter.

CHAPTER
# THIRTY-NINE

*Daniel*

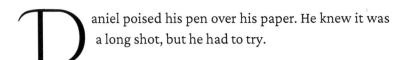aniel poised his pen over his paper. He knew it was a long shot, but he had to try.

*Dear Abigail,*

*If you've received this as I've instructed, then it's the day after we left each other at the State Capitol. I pray it will survive the years between us and get delivered. As you can imagine, writing to an address that doesn't yet exist and doesn't need to be delivered for almost 200 years will have its challenges, but I'm putting my hope in my future ancestors to carry out my wishes. I hope you realize that I'll have to get married one day and have kids. Then those kids will have to have kids, and so on and so on for several decades in order to make this delivery happen. But that's neither here nor there. It's my sincere hope that you are as happy to receive this letter as I was to think that I would be able to speak to you again by sending it. Our adventure has left me with a keen desire to do something to make this world a better place. I'm not sure what that will look like or where it will take me, but I will make sure it's a worthy endeavor (Endeavor – serious determined effort - Perhaps you'll add this to your word collection). Thank you again for our time together. I wish you many more adventures, though I think we both know that none will be as grand as the adventures of Abigail Hawk and Daniel Truly.*

*Your dearest friend,*
  *Daniel Truly*

Daniel set his pen down. Yes, that would do. That would do very well.

...SECURE COMM TRANSMISSION TO THE FANTASTIC ORDER OF ODD TRAVELERS FROM TRAVELER #2520

...RED BOOK HAS BEEN DESTROYED IN THE NC STATE CAPITOL FIRE OF 1831

...PIGGYBACK RIDER...FORMER TRAVELER...CODE NAME MAKI... LOST IN FIRE

...TARGET STATUS: ABIGAIL HAWK AND DANIEL TRULY...SECURED

...PROBABILITY OF CHANGED HISTORY: LOW

...HISTORY STATUS: PRESERVED

...23:40:03 INTERSTELLAR TIME

...CAPABILITY "CAP" BROWN

\* \* \*

...SECURE COMM TRANSMISSION TO TRAVELER #2520 FROM THE FANTASTIC ORDER OF ODD TRAVELERS

...RECEIVED

...OPERATION: COMPLETE

...RETURN HOME FOR DEBRIEF
...
...
...THE JALAPEÑO POPPERS WERE A NICE TOUCH

...23:40:05 INTERSTELLAR TIME

# Acknowledgments

...SECURE COMM TRANSMISSION TO THE
FANTASTIC ORDER OF EDITORS AT BLUE INK
PRESS FROM ONE GRATEFUL AUTHOR

...THIS BOOK COULDN'T HAVE BEEN DONE
WITHOUT YOUR AMAZING TALENT. THANK YOU
FOR ALL THE LONG HOURS YOU PUT IN TO MAKE
THIS STORY SHINE.

...FINAL THANKS TO MY ADULT CHILDREN FOR
THEIR INVALUABLE INPUT.

...OPERATION BOOK: COMPLETE

...13:25:00 EARTH TIME

# ABOUT THE AUTHOR

Sherry Torgent was born and raised in North Carolina and spent her childhood playing in the woods, riding bikes, and vying for that coveted homemade ribbon in her mother's impromptu coloring contests. Sherry is committed to writing "clean" teen fiction, and several of her young adult books have won national recognition. *The Fantastic Order of Odd Travelers* is her debut middle-grade novel.

 facebook.com/storgent
instagram.com/torgent